MEET YOUR CAST OF CHARACTERS
(all odd; some odder than others)

- Our unnamed hero: a nice, Christian, generic teenage boy
  from a generic tract house in a generic suburb
  and a generic non-denominational church,
  who learns he's "blessed" with a previously unknown "gift":
  the ability to end the world as we know it.
- A man who may or may not be a woman,
  and the woman who puts up with him.
- A businesswoman with "multiple streams of income" (all illicit),
  and her perpetually-angry business partner.
- The rainbow-robed leader of a pansexual "holy roller" orgy.
- Ménage-a-trois farmers with a plan to profit from disaster.
- An auto mechanic and part-time "energy healer."
- A couple with a big vehicle, a big house, and big secrets.
- The leader of a failing "off the grid" community
  and his dwindling, not-all-there followers.
- An old-fashioned Christian doomsday cult,
  and its aging but fiery boss.
- And most importantly (and most enigmatically,
  a cynical woman/girl with a mysterious past,
  who seems to know more about the boy
  (and what's happening to him) than he knows.

Join this bewildered young boy on a journey across state lines
and various dimensions, as he learns the secrets of the universe
and fights his pre-chosen destiny.

WHO AM I?

WHY AM I HERE?

the ERRATICA FICTION series, #2

WHO AM I? WHY AM I HERE?

A NORTHWEST NOIR ROAD NOVEL

by Clark Humphrey

SEATTLE USA

•

Thanks again to Elaine Bonow for the words of encouragement and/or exhortation, and to the members of BBC Studio Writes for important early feedback.

This is a work of fiction. Except for some of the place names, nothing in this novel really exists. I hope.

•

First edition: December 2016

ISBN (this edition): 978-1-929069-30-9

MISCmedia
1925 1st Ave., #B301
Seattle WA 98101
miscmedia.com

1.
WHAT AM I DOING HERE?
AND WHAT AM I DOING?

It's Saturday morning. The bedside clock reads 9:37.

I'd been awake and active last night even longer than I thought.

As I stand here, listening to her make small talk to me from the next room, I'm thinking about the other females in my short life.

My mother had always instructed me in the discipline of being a moral person, a righteous person, and most importantly a young man who listens and defers to women. She raised me alone from the time my father left, raised me to be the exact opposite of anything my father had been. Even to the point of her regularly making dinners of all the foods my father had always hated. (I mean, how much butternut squash and eggplant can a guy take?)

My mother had latched onto me as her self-proclaimed "last hope" for "a good child," after my older sister repeatedly proved herself to be incapable of self-discipline.

My sister was your basic Lifetime TV movie waiting to happen. One crazy or creepy boyfriend after another. The high-school dropout (while she was still in middle school). The street pot dealer. The small-time shoplifter. The steroid-hooked football star. The white slam poet with at least three other girlfriends. The hot-rod car mechanic with at least four non-working cars at any one time, and only one barely-working car. Worst of all, the English prof who'd picked her out to be his midlife-crisis temptation and "muse" for that semester.

From my mother's lessons and my sister's contrary examples, I constantly tried to be a guy who wasn't like other guys; a teen who wasn't like the other teens.

And now, here I am. A walking cliché.

I look at myself in the full-length bedroom mirror. I'd never seen myself undressed in one of these in, how long? Ever? I was never the hunkiest guy in school, or had the best posture. This sight just proves it. I look away.

It's not what I've done that I feel sad about, I decide.

I mean, what future bride (even a Christian one) expects her future husband (even a Christian one) to be "pure" anymore?

It's what I'm going to do that I'm not so sure about.

Now it's me who's the Lifetime TV movie waiting to happen.

Maybe even a "48 Hours Mystery" waiting to happen.

I look at her clothes in the closet. It's a big closet, with a lot of clothes, and an awful lot of shoes. This is the kind of woman that my mother would make snide remarks about behind her back; and maybe she'll get the chance to do so. If I'm unlucky, that is. Let's hope they never meet. My mother hasn't been to church for a while, not since before the change of pastors; so they've probably not met.

For that matter, let's hope nobody else finds out. She could go to jail for what we've done. We both could go to jail for what I'm going to do. Probably. I don't even know what it is, not really. I mean, she's said what it is, but I don't really understand it. Maybe I never will.

She's walking back in here. I stop snooping around. I close the closet doors.

No. She's still out in the other room, in this generic subdivision rambler house. Like the house I live in, it dates back to a more modest time in suburban home design, before the more recent McMansion developments.

And like the house I live in, it's not as new or as pristine as it used to be.

She's shouting at me, even though the door's open and she's no more than 20 feet away from me. She's calling me "cute" names. Yuck. She says she's writing down the driving directions. She says she's packed a lunch for me. She says there's enough gas in the car to get all the way to a place called "Scappoose" without stopping. She says I shouldn't stop. Take the bridge at Longview, then left onto Highway 30; then, when I get there, hand the keys over to the couple; they'll drive me to a bus stop. Don't stop. Don't get stopped. Don't look in the trunk. Don't let anybody else look into the trunk. Nothing she hasn't said six or seven times already.

My mother thinks I'm on a church youth-group trip.

I have a sudden thought: Has this woman done this with, or to, other guys before? I try not to think about it. I use her hairbrush.

She throws my clothes into the bedroom. They're freshly washed; still a little damp. I check: no booze or perfume or pot smell.

How'd I get here? Really easily.

As my mother had always told me to be with women, I'd been courteous, I'd been trusting, and I'd listened sympathetically to everything she'd said.

It was at this house, hers, after her husband had left for the long weekend.

We'd been exchanging texts for a few weeks. The conversation started out innocently enough. She said I'd seemed to her to be a lost soul. She offered to help me find my way in life.

But as the text exchanges went on, gradually the conversation became about her.

How she'd felt so alone, even after a year or two in this town—well, not much of a town (as she'd put it), more like a bunch of subdivisions and strip malls, connected by wide roads without sidewalks. How she'd felt like a prisoner in her own home, in her life. How she'd felt it harder and harder to keep up the smiling, optimistic public "face" she'd built for herself. How she'd needed someone to relate to, to talk to, someone honest like me, someone who kept his promises. Someone like me.

At about the time the rest of the church youth group had left town on the church's bus, I knocked on her door.

One dinner, two bottles of wine (real wine, not the grape juice our church uses in communion), and one joint later, I let her embrace me in a hug of mutual reassurance.

A half hour after that, I was in the bed I'm looking at now.

A "lesson," she'd called it. A lesson in empathy; in relating; in touching another person, body and soul. In being un-alone, at least momentarily.

Right now, though, I'm not sure about what I've really learned.

I've learned now much I was just like my older sister, whom I've strived to not be like.

I've learned how easily I could be manipulated, used for someone else's purposes.

I've learned to distrust my own carefully built sense of morality.

I feel, at least for a moment, that my life was, and is, just one big sham.

I feel fully alive; at the same time, I feel guilty for feeling that way.

I wonder how far I can run once I get dressed.

I wonder what's in the trunk.

I wonder if I could "accidentally" crash the car without hurting myself.

No, I could drive it into the river instead.

No, I'm not the greatest swimmer. And the water's too cold this time of year.

I'm still thinking about this while she yanks the hairbrush out of my hand. She's still in her robe, still barefoot with painted toenails. I remember how they'd tasted.

She opens her robe with one hand, and pushes my head toward her with the other.

Breasts, at least hers—they feel so warm and soft and taste so good, so exhilarating.

Hands, at least hers, running across my short hair—they wake up parts of my skull I didn't know could have these kinds of sensations.

I'm doing this. I'm doing all of this. Don't even think about it.

2.
WHERE AM I GOING?
AND WHO IS HE?

I can't see much through the back window of this car—just rain-drops and the silhouettes of trees and a couple of glaring outdoor lights.

But I can hear things.

I can hear at least two dogs howling and yipping.

I can hear a loud TV, coming from a building I can't see from here, playing some action movie.

I can hear the man and woman who drove me here, arguing at the top of their voices against at least one other person.

Actually, the woman isn't getting many words in. Most of the yelling's being done by her partner—boyfriend? Husband? Brother? Or is it being done by whoever the other guy inside this house is? From the way they were shouting at each other a few minutes ago, they seem to have a lot more emotionally invested in each other than you'd think mere business partners would have.

This guy, and the guy he's arguing with, sure like to drop a lot of F-bombs on each other.

I try to make out what they're saying, in between all the F-words. Even when I can make out a complete sentence, it doesn't make any sense.

At one point it almost seems as if they're trying to come up with a business deal of some kind. How much money, in what form, delivered when and where. But then they just start insulting each other again.

It's been more than half an hour since the couple left me in the back seat and told me it would just be a minute. They were sup-posed to drive me to the nearest town, where I could get a ride on a bus into Portland, and from there get back to Seattle, and from there get back to the 'burbs.

They'd made a bunch of other stops before this one, including a short stop at a gas station/convenience store, a long stop at a bar, and a longer stop at some small rural house. After they came back to the car from each of these stops, they were louder and more inco-herent and more belligerent.

Especially the man. He's about five foot one, stocky. He's got a gruff tenor voice and a face that's more "delicate" looking than his personality would imply. He's wearing an oversize black suit jacket, slacks, and a white shirt with a loosely tied tie.

The woman is a few inches taller than him, with blonde curly hair almost as short as his. She's wearing pastel slacks and a flannel shirt with very visible bra-strap lines. She's got a stern demeanor and a sharp tongue, especially toward the man. They seem to have known and loved/hated one another for some time. I'm trying to remember everything about them, in case I might have to testify someday.

It's dark now. Very dark. Cold, cloudy; threatening to rain. It's January, so it's dark when it's not even six yet. Even when I do get to the "transit center," will there be any buses still running? If I have to use my emergency-only credit card for a motel room, my mom will know I'm not at the church youth retreat I'm supposed to be at.

All my life I've tried to be the good child, the one who'd never get into any trouble or cause my mother any worry. And now I'm here, wherever this is. All I know is it's on a gravel road, off of a two-lane paved road, off of a four-lane state highway.

Every mile or so, while it was still light out, I could see a small sign posted in memory of someone who'd died in a drunk-driving crash along these roads. Each of the signs has an "In Memory Of…" phrase, a name, and a separate metal plate demanding "PLEASE DON'T DRINK AND DRIVE," and a pot of flowers by the ground. I pray to my lord Jesus that I don't become one of them.

I know I haven't been a very good Christian the past 24 hours or so, or a very good person either. I've slept with an older woman, a woman in what news stories about court trials would call "a position of trust and authority" over high-school kids like me. I've let her convince me to run a weird errand for her, driving across the state line in the same car I'm in the back seat of now, carrying I still don't know what in the trunk.

The drive was all right, considering. I'm still relatively new at the whole driving thing, so I was borderline panicky and extra careful anyway. I found this couple's place all right; even though I'd promised that woman I wouldn't use the GPS.

This other woman and this man were sort of nice when I first drove up. They didn't open the trunk or ask me anything about what was in it; they apparently knew. They instructed me to get into the back seat while they got in the front.

Outside the car now, they've stopped screaming.

Now they've started screaming again.

Now they've stopped again, and I'm hearing strange sounds from the general direction of the house, as if they're fighting. Or it could be a fight scene in the action movie on the TV. I think I hear a gunshot; but that could also be from the TV.

The dogs are even louder now.

Now the two are coming back to the car—the woman running, the man stumbling. They get in.

The woman gets in on the driver's side. She looks a little scuffed up.

But the man looks worse. He's got a bloodied hand (I hadn't noticed how skinny his fingers were until now). His suit jacket is opened; it may have lost some buttons. His shirt is opened a little too; he's got Ace bandages wrapped all around him, from the shoulders down. Was he already injured from some earlier fight?

The man and the woman say nothing. Neither do I. The woman seems even more annoyed by the man's behavior than before.

The woman finally drives us toward the nearest town, even though the man keeps grumbling at her, asking her to take him home instead.

They stop at a tiny, tired looking, line of bus stops. It looks completely deserted. The woman tells me to get out. I immediately do just that.

Then she motions for me to come toward her. She whispers to me something about how the man's "gone stupid on testosterone." I may be young, but that's sure not the first time I'd ever heard a woman complaining about testosterone and stupid men. It's something my older sister likes to say all the time, usually at the end of one of her three-week (or one-night) love affairs.

Then the woman tells me I should have seen the man "before." I don't ask her what she means.

She quickly drives off back in the direction we'd come from.

According to the signs I find the bus stop (officially a "transit center") has indeed had its last departure of the night.

In the alley behind the bus stop, I hear some teenagers screaming and clinking bottles together. One of the voices sounds vaguely familiar.

3.
WHO ARE THEY?
HOW DO I DEAL WITH THEM?

The alley behind the closed bus-transfer station is about the only even vaguely "city" looking thing in this little town. The town's name, from a sign on the bus station's side, is "St. Helens."

A town with the same name as America's most active volcano, just across the river and the state line from here. If it were daylight and clear, I might be able to see its hollowed-out cone from here.

This street and this alley look like nothing's "gone off" in it in a long, long time.

There are a dozen or more teenagers and young adults standing around in this alley. They're drinking beer and Southern Comfort. They're smoking both kinds of cigarettes.

It's not so much that I joined up with them, but more that they surrounded and engulfed me. I heard them. Then they saw me. Then they decided to bring me into their little scene.

Even though I'm pretty clearly not one of them.

One drunken guy's been calling me "Mr. Peter Perfect Boy Scout." A girl who's high on something (I don't know what) keeps calling me "White-Ass," even though they're all white themselves. A guy with a circle-A on his leather jacket calls me "Mr. Conformity," even though they're all like one another and I'm the only "different" one here.

But I've learned a lot of people don't understand what my life-style and my religion mean to me. I'm not trying to "fit in" with the other kids in my school. I stand out from them, in fact. Not just because I don't (or didn't until just recently) drink, smoke, swear, or sleep around; but because I try to be a good student and a good person, not just to have "fun" and get by.

Our former pastor used to say "true" Christians weren't really the "mainstream" of American society. The real mass population, he said, consisted of secular, materialistic people who pretended to follow some watered-down idea of Christianity. He said that we, the "true Christians," were the only wide-awake people in a world full of sleepwalkers.

Which is more or less what these kids are saying about themselves, as opposed to me. They're claiming that they're "woke" and people like me are "in the Matrix."

One reason I liked our former pastor is he wasn't afraid to use "big words." I try not to use long words in public. I don't want people to think I'm too "weird." Of course, that's just what these people here think of me.

My current co-pastor couple wouldn't pass judgment on these kids; they're just not like that. But my old pastor would have. He'd have said they were unknowing slaves to drink, drugs, bad music, bad attitudes, and (worst of all) to the adolescent curse of sex madness.

It was my own sex drive that first got me into this mess. And now I'm even deeper into the mess. Whatever it is.

My youth-group leader, who's also my male co-pastor, always says we've always got choices to make. We can choose to let emotions and obsessions control us, or we can choose to control them. We can choose the way of selfishness and greed, or we can choose the way of compassion and love.

The female co-pastor doesn't say much about sex, except that it's a healthy and God-given gift that we shouldn't spend "wastefully." She's talked about getting and staying out of abusive relationships; about not getting emotionally caught up too far with another kid who was just as immature as you were; and about not getting, or getting anyone, pregnant. But she's never told us to never do it.

Which, according to these "street kids" (do any of them live "on the streets" or are they just having a night out?) is what I'll soon have to do.

They've collectively decided I need to be converted from what one guy's calling "Mr. Goody Two Shoes" into someone more like them. The girls are playing an old playground game to decide which of them will be the first to corrupt me. I don't tell them I've already been corrupted, by someone I'd trusted. I don't tell them much of anything.

The guy with the circle-A jacket tells me if I let them do this "to" me, they'll then do something "for" me. "What did you want for Christmas that you didn't get?" I presume that means they'll shove a bottle or a joint into my hand. I mumble that I just want to get home.

"Done!," he proclaims. I haven't told him how far away home is for me. Right now it seems like a million years away.

The girl who won the playground game walks toward me in a pseudo-stripper strut, in an opened jacket and dirty jeans and jet-black earrings. Here in the dark, she alternately looks either no older than 15 or prematurely aged. She lifts her T-shirt (just a T-shirt under a jacket, in January?). She grabs my right hand and pulls it onto her left breast. She tells me it's time for me to be a man. It turns out it was she who, from outside the closed bus station, I thought sounded like someone who used to be in my youth group. I don't recognize her face, not in this dark place.

She gives me a brief but aggressive kiss. Her breath DOESN'T smell as if she'd been drinking or smoking (anything).

Now she's reaching to my pants zipper, as she kneels to the pavement. I didn't think she'd really do this. I really didn't think the rest of the kids would gather in to watch.

Even though I (really) don't want to respond, my body does anyway. It's over mercifully soon. She wipes herself off with my shirt-tail.

How I feel right now: just weird.

In my body, I've never felt so "manly" before (not even last night).

In my mind and emotions, I'm confused. I'm embarrassed. I'm disgusted, mostly at myself, mostly because I didn't hate it as much as I'm supposed to. There's even a part of me that likes having been the center of attention.

I realize I still haven't eaten since a sack lunch in the car this afternoon. If they make me drink with them, I'll really be in trouble.

They make me drink with them. Southern Comfort, straight from the bottle. A lot of it. I try not to throw up. I fail.

My ordeal is cut short by the headlights of a car driving into the alley. It's the same car I came here in. But somebody else is driving.

4.
WHAT AM I?
WHAT ARE THEY?

It's tomorrow. Just barely, but tomorrow anyway.

And already, things are getting better for me. Just barely, but better anyway.

My first solid food in more than 12 hours is in my right hand. It's a large hot beef burrito, straight from the convenience-store microwave. Before I eat it, I let its warmth touch both sides of both my hands and the lower half of my face. My new Fred Meyer jacket isn't keeping all of the wee-hours January coldness away from me.

Above me, I can see a lot of stars that I normally don't get to see in the heart of suburbia. But they're shining clearly down on this lonely rural highway.

Below me, the rest of my very late dinner sits waiting in a white paper bag on this little moat of sidewalk in front of the store. A bag of Flaming Cheetos, a bottled Frappuccino, a Slim Jim jerky stick, and a lidded cup of coffee with non-dairy creamer.

My mother would kill me if she saw me consuming all of this. Hell, she'd kill me if she knew any of what I'd done a few hours ago and what I'd done the night before, and what I very well might do today—even though I don't know what that will be.

My mother's always repeats whatever she hears from the TV doctors and reads on the parenting blogs. Every item in this "meal," and probably every ingredient in every item in it, falls well within any of those sources' lists of things to never feed to a growing boy ever.

But it tastes so good right now, as I bite into it. The white tortilla wrap. The melted cheese product just inside the wrap, just outside the main filling of textured, seasoned beef with who-knows-what-else as filler. It's filling. It's satisfying. It even smells welcoming.

Can something this supposedly disgusting also be so delicious, so just-what-I-needed-right-now?

In front of me is the girl who'd jumped into the car with me, from the alley behind the bus station a couple of towns back. The same girl who apparently believes, mistakenly, that she'd de-virginized me.

I still swear I've heard her voice before, from somebody who used to be in my youth group at the church. But she doesn't look like any girl I knew or ever would have known.

She's talking with a woman, one of the two people who were in the car when they picked me up in the alley.

It's the same car I'd driven down in, carrying who-knows-what in the trunk across state lines. As far as I know, it could have been anything from drugs to a dead body.

The girl and the woman are talking almost too fast for me to make out all of what they're saying. But I "fine tune" my hearing in my head, and then I can hear them, though not necessarily understand them.

The girl apparently used to be involved in some sort of work with the woman, who's inviting her back into whatever it is. The woman asks if the girl remembers how much money she'd made, how much fun she'd had.

The woman's asking the girl to remember when she was buying the best clothes and the best weed, working just a few hours a day, with the woman always there to keep her safe. The woman asks if the girl remembered that she'd even gotten to go to that big outdoor music festival.

The girl turns away from the woman, then back toward her. The girl looks to the woman's side, then at her. The girl says she'd loved having all that money to spend, sure, but she now wishes she'd have saved some of it. The girl then says that yes, her time working for the woman was fun, and profitable, and exciting, and taught her a lot about herself. But now she wants a different "life" than "the life."

About 20 feet away from me, the man who's been driving the car is opening the trunk now, just in front of the gas pumps. I lean forward to try to get a look. All I can see in there now is some clear plastic tarp and one small, old-fashioned satchel bag. The driver, whose name I haven't learned yet, is taking the bag out and closing the trunk.

Now he's trying to grab the nozzle from the gas pump. But he can't. It's locked somehow. The clerk from the store runs out. Now the driver and the clerk are arguing. "What do you mean there's no pumping your own gas in this state?" This means the driver's probably a Washingtonian, like me. And like me, he's stuck down here in Nowhere, Oregon on some fool's errand or another. And unlike me, he probably at least knows why he's here.

But why is the driver acting so belligerent with this clerk (a guy who can't be that much older than me; probably just old enough to legally sell beer)? Over some silly state law that this clerk's not allowed to break, no matter how loudly the clerk gets yelled at?

What's the point? There isn't any. So why's the driver yelling? Is he on something? If he is, or even if he isn't, do I dare get back into the car with him? And if I don't, then what do I do?

His voice, while he's arguing, sounds at least a little like the voice from inside the country house where that other man, the one I'd originally turned the car over to, went in. Come to think of it, I could only hear that voice because they were arguing so loudly.

This man had been quiet during the 15-minute drive from the alley to wherever this is. I was too tired to keep my eyes open to see any road signs.

Now that I've got a little food in me (though my mother would call it something other than "food"), I feel a little more awake. The coffee and the Frappuccino will surely help this a little more.

As my brain gets back into gear, at least a little, I try to remember how I got into this situation in the first place.

I'd turned down the woman who'd become my first lover at first, in texts. No, even before "at first." I'd said I had things to do and couldn't join her for coffee. Then I'd said I didn't want to hear her sad tales of woe about "a friend" who needed a simple act of Christian charity. Then I'd said I didn't want to go to her house. Then I'd said I didn't want to share her wine. Then I'd said I didn't want to dance with her to the music of that techno-pop diva on Spotify.

I'd told her how my former pastor listed "dancing" pretty high up on his list of things all good Christian "teens" were supposed to never do. Right along with drinking, smoking, "necking," disobeying the church, disobeying your parents, wearing pants (for girls), and a lot of other things.

Then she (the particular "she" who got me into all this) said the previous pastor's idea of a good Christian sounded like he'd have thought a coma patient would be the greatest saint there ever was.

She said being a good Christian, or a good person in general, wasn't about what you didn't do. It was about what you DID do. It was about helping people, caring about people, making a difference in this world.

She said I was using the idea of "good" as an excuse to be passive, to stay in my own "comfort zone," to avoid doing anything that a truly good person dares to do.

My brain isn't quite back up to speed yet, so I can't quite remember how that train of logic led to me being in her arms, then being in her bed, then being in her car, then being here now. But, somehow, it did.

The man at the car, meanwhile, is still arguing with the clerk about a state law here that the clerk can't do anything about, and also about a few other things that didn't even happen at this store, just somewhere in what the man calls this backwards state.

The woman from the car sees me staring at the man. She says there are reasons she stays with him; reasons a nice Mormon boy wouldn't understand. I don't bother to tell her that I'm not Mormon, I'm Calvary Fellowship. Even in my hometown, most people haven't heard of our still-little church, albeit a little church with plans to become big.

The girl, still standing to one side of the woman, says nothing, but looks as though she seems to know what at least some of those reasons the woman stays with the man are. As I've been doing all night so far, I don't ask.

The store clerk finally finishes pumping the gas, re-locking the pump, and taking cash from the man in wadded-up bills.

Before the man can get into the car, the woman runs up and gets into the driver's seat. I get in the back, with the girl. The woman promises to help me get home. But we pull off back in the direction we'd come from.

The girl sees that I'm weary. She offers me what she says is a wake-up pill, "as safe as coffee." I accept it, but I place it in my pocket for now.

5.
AT LEAST I KNOW WHERE I AM.
OR DO I?

I'm out of the car again. I'm on the side of a lonely county high-way. About twenty feet from me, there's a signpost with a flowerpot and a reflecting metal sign in memory of someone who'd apparently been run down by a drunk driver. It's like several signs I'd seen ear-lier tonight, or last night. The sign "lights up" when a car with its high beams on passes it. The girl beside me says there's one of those about every mile or so on these roads. I just hope nobody ends up putting one of them up for me.

There are no streetlights.

There are no sidewalks—just a narrow strip of grass between the pavement and a deep ditch. I have to step carefully when a car passes on my side.

The few drivers here, at this time of night, don't pay attention to the potential presence of any people standing or walking. They don't pay attention to the speed limits either.

Most of the time, when there's not a car coming or going, it's real-ly really dark here. High clouds are gathering in the big sky above me, hiding the stars I could see less than an hour ago.

I've been surrounded by darkness for nine hours now and I'm still alive, still awake, and still alert, though I'm also still lost.

The darkness. That's what our old pastor said we had to always prepare for. He always said the world was going into a time of great tribulation, any day now. He said it even more often whenever a Democrat was in, or threatening to get into, the White House.

He said we had to be always aware, always ready. Our spiritual "houses" had to always be in order. Because when the Rapture came and the End Times began, only the truest of the true believers, with the purest of pure souls and the most sinless of sinless lives, would be chosen.

Who wouldn't be chosen: The unbelievers. The heathen. The druggies, the hippies and yippies, the fornicators, and the "per-verts." The materialistic masses who only pretended to believe in some faint imitation of Christianity. The members of churches that got the Gospel wrong or added things to it (Mormons, Catholics, and most others). Even if what they got wrong was some tiny, tiny point of doctrine or policy or Scripture interpretation, such as how many days Jesus was "dead" before His resurrection—they were all damned.

The old pastor kept saying this right up to the day he lost control of the Calvary Fellowship Ministry, in what some ex-members called a "palace coup" by the board of deacons. Where he went to after that, nobody seems to know. Maybe he was Raptured.

I have only a little more of an idea about where I am now. Before we'd stopped, I'd caught sight of a road sign. We're apparently somewhere between Beaver Springs and Trojan Park. I tell this to the girl. She makes a dirty joke of it, naturally.

In the darkness, where I can't see her prematurely aged face, I realize where I remember her voice. She'd been a couple grades ahead of me in school—not quite as old as my older sister. She'd been in my church. Her family was one of the ones that quit after the old pastor got fired. That family, and several of the others who left the church, also moved out of town, apparently in search of a new church that would be just as strict as their old one used to be.

Don't remember her name, though.

Why is she here? (For that matter, why am I here?)

I ask the first real question I've asked of anybody this strange night.

I ask her name.

She tells it.

No, it doesn't strike any memories in me. At least not right away.

But then again, I have been known for withdrawing into my head a lot, pretty much all my life. It sure hasn't helped me make friends at school, or dates.

We talk a little more. Just about small stuff. Like how cold it is out right now, and when the woman and man who drove us up here in the car, then stopped and got out, will ever come back.

I don't ask what this job she'd had with the woman (and possibly the man) was.

I don't ask what the man and woman are doing wherever they disappeared to off the road.

She tells me a few things anyway. Maybe she can tell how lost, how confused, I am.

But she doesn't tell them completely. She apparently assumes I know even just a little about my own present situation, which I really don't. (But I don't tell her that.)

She says the woman and man are into what the woman once told her were "multiple streams of income." That means, the girl says, that they've got a lot of fingers in a lot of candy jars. She calls the woman her mother sometimes (even though she really isn't); her sister some other times; but mainly she just calls her "Pseudo-Mom." She just calls the man by his first name. Tonight, the girl says, they're making a deal with someone she called by a nickname I never heard of, but who seems to be somebody they all know. It's apparently connected to some other deal earlier that fell through or went south. That might be the altercation I saw earlier tonight, elsewhere along this or some other nearby road.

After what seems like forever but is really just 20 minutes (according to the cell phone I only turn on for brief moments; I don't dare let its battery die), the woman and man emerge from a dark gravel driveway. They're jogging back toward the stopped car they'd parked at the head of the driveway. In the darkness I can't see their faces very well. But from their body language, they don't seem to be particularly upset or angry (in the man's case, at least not more angry than he'd seemed before).

We get back into the car. The girl (well, she's really a young woman, and looks from some angles like an early-middle-aged woman) is with me in the back seat, as before.

As we pull back onto the road, I briefly turn my cell phone back on and check our location. We're less than 20 miles from the bridge where I'd crossed the state line so many hours ago. But we're traveling further away from there.

When I power down my phone and stick it back into my pocket, the girl leans over to me.

She tells me I should take that pep pill she'd already given me.

She whispers that she knows who I am and why I'm here. (The last part is more than I know right now.) She "proves it" my calling me by my name, which I'm pretty sure I hadn't told her yet.

Then she says she'll protect me. But she doesn't say from what.

6.
WHERE IS THIS?
WHEN IS THIS?

It's really quiet in here. I may get scared of the quiet later on, but for now it's a relief. "I can finally hear myself think," to borrow one of my mother's pet phrases.

Damn I miss her. Even if we disagree about a lot of things, she's always there for me. Except now; but that's not her fault.

I wonder if she's thinking about me now? As far as she knows, I'm at a church youth-group retreat this MLK Day weekend. She expects me to walk in the door at home a day and a half from now, maybe tired, wearing dirty clothes, but otherwise rested and inspired to be a better person.

She stopped going to church after the divorce. Was I still in grade school then? I think so. I still don't blame her. The old women at that church, under its old pastor, used to be very judgmental about spouses, especially wives, who abandoned the ol' 'til-death-us-do-part business. Even if those wives had really good reasons.

I know people drift apart from one another. My older sister has left, or been left by, more boyfriends than I can count. My mother herself never remarried, though she came close a couple of times.

The woman and man who'd just been in the car with me seem to be of a different type—the type of couples who can't stand each other but can't live without each other either. In Calvary Fellowship we don't believe in "purgatory" or divide Hell into "circles;" but if we did, a relationship like that would certainly qualify as one of those.

Ever since that girl and I got back into the car back out by Beaver Springs Road, the woman (who drove the car this most recent leg) and the man were arguing. They didn't get tremendously loud. But they also didn't stop. They accused each other of betraying something they both claimed to care about. The "right," they called it. Or was it the "rite"?

Even worse, they had the car radio on that late night conspiracy theory and ghost story talk show. When they weren't yapping at each other, they were listening to the radio guy yapping about some new cult group and its new prophecy for this new age. The cult apparently says the "awakened" or "woke" peoples of Earth, the people who reject the New World Order's agenda of destruction, are about to "ascend into a higher frequency" that will cause them to rise beyond the plane of what we think of as physical existence. Just like the Mayans and other peoples of history had done.

This sounds a lot like a different interpretation of what our former pastor used to preach about all the time. The End Times. The Darkness.

It would start with the Rapture, in which the pure, the true believers, would be "harvested" from this life. Then would come seven years of Hell on Earth, led by the Antichrist, which our old pastor described as both Satan incarnate and as the ultimate communist liberal, who'd impose a United Nations One World Government to persecute everybody and confiscate everybody's guns. Then after all that, the Messiah would descend from Heaven again and sort the Heaven-bound from the Hell-bound.

I didn't say anything about this in the car. As I'm telling the girl from the car now, I'm still operating on the principle of trying not to get myself further into trouble. The girl says I'm getting further into trouble anyway, so my silence isn't working. I don't try to contest her on this.

She and I are out of the car again. It feels good.

Now, the car's not objectively a bad place to be. It's a nice late-model white import sedan, with most of the modern convenience options. Metal and glass on the outside; various kinds of plastic on the inside. No dents, scratches, torn seats, or cracked windows. An engine that starts when it's supposed to; brakes that stop when they're supposed to. A working heater. If I didn't feel so helpless, it would be what my more car-crazy friends would call "a nice ride." I try to praise the Lord even under trying circumstances, so I silently thank Him for my relative safety and comfort this weird night.

And that includes the place where I am now.

It's an old house. It's run down, and it's cold, but it's shelter.

It's starting to rain outside. I can hear a leaky ceiling somewhere in another room.

The man and woman who'd been driving the car have deposited the girl and I here, then driven off. They didn't say where they were going or when, or if, they'd be back. And I didn't ask.

I'm not going to check where I am on the cell phone, not with its battery this low. I tried to recharge it, but there's no electricity here.

There is running water, cold. I wash my face and hands at the kitchen sink, and dry myself off with a tablecloth.

I feel beard stubble on my chin. Not much, but some.

I finally take the pep pill the girl had given me, and wash it down with more water from the tap.

I take a deep breath, then another. These breaths, and the rain and the leak, are the only sounds I hear for a moment, until the girl's footsteps resume along the creaky wood floor.

It's dark in here, so I can't really see the premature wrinkles on her face or the weird spot on her lower lip. She stands up straight as she walks toward me, with a confident stride I don't remember seeing among the girls my own age.

She talks to me, in what might as well be riddles.

A few of the things she says I understand. Like when she says she needs to start making money again, but not so much that she can afford to get back on the bad drugs. And when she says weed's OK but meth will drain the life force from you. She says the "F-word" several times during this.

She talks about the woman in the car, whom she calls her "Pseudo-Mom." She doesn't say just what line of work she'd been in with the woman. But from the hints she drops, it was probably an illegal thing, maybe even several illegal things. (I remember her previous remark about "multiple streams of income.") She says she hates Pseudo-Mom sometimes, but can't seem to break away from her.

She says only a few things about the man in the car. Apparently he and Pseudo-Mom are only business partners, not lovers. She says the man has an ex-wife he's still in love with, even though she's "a totally different person these days."

But she also says a lot of things I don't get at all.

Like when she says I'm not really as prepared as I ought to be for what's coming next. She says "they" (the man and woman from the car? Somebody else?) won't "be easy" on me. I've got to make myself psyched up for "the induction."

I ask her what "the induction" is.

She just laughs, telling me I already know what it is. Which I don't.

Otherwise, as I've done all night, I say little to nothing. I sure don't tell her much about myself. Compared to her, I live (or lived, until the night before yesterday) a very dull, "normal" life in a clean-cut subdivision. I get good grades in school, but not great. I don't know what I want to study in college. I don't have a girlfriend. I've got a sister who's now in what used to be called a "community" college. I've got a mom with a decent enough job at a bank branch.

Why would I tell her this? She'd probably just scoff at me, and she'd tell me (with a few "F-words" interspersed) that I don't know how the world really works.

After a moment of awkward silence, I sit down on a tired old overstuffed sofa, one of the few pieces of furniture in here. She follows me.

I try to think about what to do next. I know it's just a short hike back to civilization, to a ride home, or a cop to report to. At least back to the convenience store, where I can call a cab or an Uber if they run this late, or hang out inside until dawn if they don't.

As what the old pastor used to call "a strapping young lad" (not really the most athletic guy in school, but hearty enough), I know I'd have the stamina to make the hike, even on no sleep. The girl presumably knows the way. I can ask her for directions even if she doesn't want to hike with me.

Then it starts raining. Hard. The leak elsewhere in the house gets loud and steady, like a ticking grandfather clock.

I lie back on the sofa.

Her pep pill sure isn't giving me any pep.

My mind gets fuzzy. The sofa feels so soft. I don't even mind how cold it is.

7.
WHY DO I DO THAT?
AND WHERE ARE MY PANTS?

I briefly come to. It's still dark.

I sense that I'm cold, and that something itches, and that something's either wrong or merely weird about my condition. But I'm too weary to amass the thinking power to sort it out any further.

And how could I have gotten so tired from a day and night of sitting (albeit for a long time) in car seats, interspersed with standing around and watching other people doing and saying things?

I don't think very hard about that, either, before I go "under" again.

When I awaken for good, it's the daytime; such as it is on an overcast mid-January day. I slowly open my eyes.

There's a thin, scruffy-feeling blanket on top of me. I feel its slight itch from my chest to my toes.

Wait a minute.

My clothes: where are they?

I'm pretty sure I was wearing them when I dozed off on this stinky old sofa.

No, I KNOW I was wearing them then.

I can't run out of here in the rain, barefoot, wearing only a blanket, now can I? (Though that would make it more probable that I'd attract the local police, who could help me to get home from all this.)

The living room of this abandoned house, in the light, looks just as decrepit as it felt when I first got here in the middle of the wee hours. There's peeling wallpaper on the walls, in some sickly looking ornate floral pattern. There's flaky white paint (probably lead-based) on the windowsills. The small front windows lie behind busted blinds. There's a bare wooden floor with one dirty oval rug on it. There's no art on the walls, though there is a rectangular light spot along a wall where something might have been.

I wrap the blanket around me as I stand up. I approach one of the windows and look beneath the broken slats of the shades. Yep, it's still raining out, but not as heavily as earlier in the night.

There seem to be stains along this floor. Don't know what they're from.

I walk to the door and open it. I look around. No visible marks of human activity, except the gravel driveway that disappears into the trees. I turn to look at the front of the house. It's covered in a hideous brown fake-brick pattern (made of what—tar?), that's flaking away around the edges.

I take one step onto the creaky small wooden porch. My bare foot immediately recoils from the wet cold.

I turn back inside. Still no electricity. Can't recharge my phone here. If I can even find my phone.

I rummage through the mostly empty kitchen. Is there any food in this abandoned claptrap? Just half a box of stale crackers, a can of tuna fish (without a can opener), and one wrinkled old potato.

The (cold only) running water still works, like it did last night. I drink up straight from the tap.

There's a battery-operated clock in the kitchen I hadn't noticed last night. If it's correct (and there's no reason to believe it either is or isn't), it's nearly noon. There's only eight and a half hours of daylight this time of year, and I've missed almost half of it. I've got to find my way out of wherever this nowhere is, preferably before dark. But now I'll also need to find shoes, and my phone. Oh, and my pants. And my shirt and jacket, if I don't want to get pneumonia.

In the bathroom, with the leaky ceiling whose sound I've somehow sent back into the background of my brain, the toilet works. I use it. I wash my hands and face again. I put the blanket back around me before I leave the room. I suppose I could walk around in here without it. Nobody else is here, right?

Wait, wasn't somebody else here last night?

Yes. There was the girl. I keep calling her that in my head, even though she's at least two or three years older than me, and from some angles looks even older than that. Why do I think of her as a girl? I guess it's just that she acts like a teenager so much. Spoiled, then pouty, then petulant, then overemotional. Everything (well, some of the things) I've tried to not be, sometimes more successfully than other times.

So. The girl: where is she?

There's not many other places in this house for either her or my stuff to be.

I go to the parts of the house I hadn't gone to last night. Basically there's just a hallway, a closet, a small bedroom, and a smaller bedroom. There's nothing in any of them but a small wooden chair and one half-unmade bed. So that's where the blanket came from. I decide to use the white bed sheet (which, like the blanket, has seen better days) as my next makeshift robe.

I untie the itchy blanket. The exact moment it drops to the floor is the moment the girl walks into the room. She snickers at me. Would she like it if some guy did that to her? I bet not! I almost tell her off but don't.

Before I can snap at her, she tells me to hurry up and follow her out in back of the house.

I tie up the bed sheet and dart out. I let each bare foot stay on the cold wet ground for as few fractions of a second as is physically possible.

She leads me into a little garage in back of the house. (When did anybody ever build one-car garages, on lots where they had room to build bigger ones?) She's still dressed as she was last night: tight designer jeans with a knee patch, generic sneakers, a black and white T-shirt with the slogan OUT OF YOUR LEAGUE (the latter word in baseball-jersey script), a short fake-leather jacket, short-cropped black hair, solid black earrings.

The concrete floor here in the garage isn't much warmer than the ground between here and the house. Thankfully, she soon shows me to the spot in here where she'd hid my clothes. She makes no attempt to turn away as I clumsily put my underwear and pants on under the bed sheet. I undo, and then step onto, the sheet. I put on my shirt, windbreaker jacket, socks, and shoes.

Everything that had been in my pockets is still in them.

She asks me to forgive her for taking my clothes. She says she was afraid I'd try to leave without her (which, indeed, I would have). She says again that I need her, and I'm supposed to know it. There seems to be a lot she thinks I'm supposed to know.

I'd been brought up to never talk rude to a woman. But now, I do. I look her in the eye. I tell her to stop talking in riddles already and tell me exactly, plainly, what she said she knows about why I'm here.

"But you KNOW why," she insists.

"No I DON'T," I insist right back.

She takes a step back, leaning against a wall. She lights up a (tobacco) cigarette, from a pack she'd fished out from a pocket in her jacket. It's the same brand my mother used to smoke before she quit; the one that was supposed to be made by Native Americans but really wasn't, and was supposed to be "good for you" but really wasn't. She apologizes for doing this; she says it's the last drug she hasn't kicked yet, not completely.

Then she asks, "Where do I (F-word) start?"

"How about at the beginning?"

She proceeds to start from the beginning, or at least from "a" beginning.

The story she tells is a really confusing one. It includes a lot of "F-words" in weird parts of her sentences. She talks about the "woke people," the "freaks," the "elevated ones," the nonconformists, the ones who reject this world's limits on who they can be. She talks about energy healing, vibrational frequencies, and the ancient Mayans.

She asks me if I've heard of the "holy rollers."

Of course, I tell her. The Pentecostals, the churches where people "speak in tongues." My own church had apparently been one of those once, before my now ex-pastor took it in a stricter direction.

No, she says. The original "holy rollers" were a group that had started in a town about eighty miles south of here about a hundred years ago, or so she says. They were called the "holy rollers" because they spent a lot of time rolling around on the floor in some sort of religious orgasm. And they were mostly women, she adds; some of them married women.

But that group's preacher got into big trouble because, as she puts it, "he couldn't keep his (F-word) (D-word) in his pants." The husbands and brothers of his female worshippers got him jailed for adultery, which was something you could do then. After he got out, one of those guys shot him. Then one of the women later shot the guy who'd shot him.

I tell her I'm sure that's a great story, but what does it have to do with me?

She starts to say something about people these days who have looked into these old stories, "not just because they're great (F-word) true stories but because they think those old people were onto something."

Before she can say much more, I hear a car approaching on the gravel driveway. From in here I can't see it, but it sounds like it might be a different car from the one that had brought me here. Car doors open and close. Two or more sets of footsteps approach.

8.
WHAT KIND OF PLACE IS THIS?
WHAT'S GOING ON HERE?

It seems like we've been driving forever, but it's only been an hour and 45 minutes on the minivan's dash clock. I'm still wheezy from whatever knockout drug the girl had slipped me. Would she like it if some guy did that to her?

(Perhaps, with what little she's told me about her own life, some guy had done it, or something like it, to her. She sure seems to have had a rough life in any event.)

And what's her interest in keeping me in the custody of these people anyway? And what do they want with me to begin with? She's been silent about that in the back seat of this minivan during this drive.

In the front seat, the woman the girl calls "Pseudo-Mom" is at the wheel. The angry man whom the girl calls Pseudo-Mom's business partner is riding shotgun. Pseudo-Mom is also mostly silent, except when she occasionally feels the need to stop the man beside her from starting or resuming grumbling arguments with the man in the middle seat. He's the man I'd originally delivered the other car to, a little over 24 hours ago that seems like a million years.

He's wearing a different slightly oversized suit jacket with matching slacks, and a different loose fitting shirt. He's got about as little beard stubble as I've got; but it's on a chin and cheekbones that look, in profile, narrow, even slightly dainty.

He and the man in the front seat sure seem to have a lot of past history with each other. Off and on all along this drive, they've been grumbling to each other about past events and present character flaws. The man in the middle seat says at one point that becoming who he is (whatever that means) had nothing directly to do with getting away from the man in the front seat; it's just that he'd really needed to do both.

At least two or three times this trip, the woman beside this man in the middle seat (the same woman who'd been with him when I first met him) nudged him with her right elbow. On one of those occasions, she quietly but sternly reprimanded him for his attitude. She "reminded" him that they were supposed to be on a spiritual journey today, a trip of unity and positivity. He simply grumbled some inarticulate-to-me cuss words.

I'd long since given up any hope or illusion that these people would get me home, or in the direction of home, or that they even wanted to. They seem to have an agenda for me. Even if they won't tell me what it is, beyond code words about "the induction" and "the great ascending."

Even now that we've gotten here.

Wherever "here" is.

The minivan didn't have its GPS unit on, if it had one. We'd stayed away from any freeways, going down a succession of wide and narrow county roads. The window on my side kept getting steamed up, no matter how many times I tried to wipe it off with my hands and sleeves. Even when I could see outside, from that window or from the front, I didn't see much that would say where we were. An endless stream of roads, trees, wheat and corn fields, houses, gas stations, mini marts, ugly modern grade schools, roadside burger joints and wine bars, main streets of small towns I'd never heard of with signs promoting the local Rotary Club, rustic old churches that reminded me of my church back home, signs for a corn maze and U-pick pumpkins, few other cars, fewer other people.

The minivan's audio system played a CD of New Age instrumentals that were, I guess, supposed to be "chill out" material. When that ended, Pseudo-Mom stuck in some generic drum n' bass, which the girl beside me visibly preferred. She boogied in her seat belt the rest of the way to here.

"Here" is a large, more or less circular, clearing with trees on all sides, at the end of another gravel road. Other vehicles had been parked here before we arrived, and more have arrived since.

The driving machines here include generic late-model sedans and pickups; one beater VW bus with a "burning man" logo decal; a couple of luxury cars with rainbow-flag bumper stickers; an old beater Volvo; a few Priuses ("Pri-i"?); and one short, converted, and repainted former school bus.

The people from some of these vehicles have built "tailgate party"-like food and drink setups. Some of them are relatively elaborate. Some have gas BBQ grills cooking chicken and hot dogs (some of them "veggie dogs") under awnings in case of rain (which has been off and on all day), with camper coolers full of beer and soft-drink cans on ice. Others simply serve coffee from big cardboard dispenser boxes and bags of Doritos from the backs of station wagons.

Before I can take advantage of these people's hospitality, a woman hands me a large paper cup of coffee. She says it's got soy milk and what she says is "special natural sugar." It makes the coffee sweet enough, I suppose, but with a weird taste added.

(My mother went through a phase of hating anything with refined sugar, but gorged on things with "natural" sugar. But that "natural" sugar didn't look exactly like this does.)

I eat just about anything I can. Several pieces of chicken. A bratwurst. A couple handfuls of "natural" cheese puffs. A veggie kebab (the one thing that comes halfway to close to something my mother would approve of).

(My mother always said I was a typical teenage boy with "a bottomless stomach." I'd always devoured big dinner portions, while she was on one fad diet after another and my big sister was on one "socially conscious" eating regimen after another.)

Around some of the other vehicles, people seem to be having shots of liquor or pre-mixed cocktails, popping who knows what kinds of pills, smoking cannabis joints and who knows what else. One could make a small fortune selling drugs to this crowd. Maybe that's what my four adult riding companions have been doing; or maybe they're doing something else.

Other people here are doing simple exercises and yoga poses, greeting one another with hugs and kisses and (in a couple of cases) serious making out. Not all of the couples making out are of opposite sexes.

There are about 40 or 50 people here now. They look like a cross section of everyone my former pastor said would be going to Hell, and then some. There are 70-year-old hippies with long gray hair. Middle aged punks and "burners." Young ravers and (white and Asian) hip hoppers. Gays, lesbians, and who-knows-whats. A few "normal looking" people, who seem to be the biggest joint smokers. Very few children, mostly under-fives. There's even one Black couple here, looking way overdressed. (Yes, this is MLK Day weekend, and these are the first African Americans I've seen on this trip. But I am in either the whitest or second-whitest state in the union, after all.)

I think I see some of the people I'd seen in that alley the second night of this misadventure. But since it was so dark there back then, I'm not sure.

One to four at a time, they're closing down whatever they've been doing at their own or other people's vehicles. They walk up another gravel road at the back end of this clearing. This particular place seems to be just a parking lot for whatever's back there, hidden by the trees and the late-afternoon fog.

Soon enough, the two women from the minivan announce it's time for us to head in and get ready (for what?). The two men follow them. The girl does likewise, physically pushing me from the back to walk off with them.

I don't have to walk far before we turn a curve in the path and I see where we're going. It's a large tent, like the ones my old pastor used to hold revival meetings in. Some people are carrying benches and outdoor propane heaters into it.

Beside the front of the tent, a woman in a multi-colored robe (a "coat of many colors," as it were) waves to our group. She looks familiar somehow.

Wait: I know.

No. It can't be.

No. It is.

Outside the tent, the sky's changing quickly from overcast to just dark.

Here inside the tent, what light we've been getting from the outside is fading, leaving candles and generator-powered lamps, and little Christmas tree-like lights strung from below the tent's ceiling.

This is all going way too quickly, too intensely.

It's amazingly loud in here.

Even more amazingly, what had been a cacophony of disparate noises is meshing in my brain into a single, somehow harmonious, blend, like some avant-garde symphony.

It gets more intense every minute.

At its base line, there's a sampled track of "chill-out" electronic music, with a steady thumping beat, coming from a portable sound system.

In the aisles, women in clothing ranging from flowing white robes to almost nothing are rolling and writhing, screaming and moaning.

In the back of the tent, various people are dancing, swaying, and kissing. Some of them might even be having sex back there, but I can't see that far in the increasing dark.

On the benches, people are standing or lying down. Almost nobody's sitting except some of the 70-year-old hippies. They're howling and chanting and "om"-ing.

I'm trying my hardest to stay attentive, alert, sane, untaken by this. Almost everything my church upbringing taught me to hate is here before my unbelieving eyes.

Just in front of me, at the front of the little stage platform, the leader of this "induction service" shouts and sings her "sermon" points.

I'd been briefly shocked when I first saw her here, in her rainbow robes. A beaming late-middle-aged lady, with a huge flower in her streaked hair. She has large eyeglasses, and a cane she seems to use only as a prop. She seems to exude a kind of half-creepy "warmth" from her very pores.

How did one of the people from my church, who'd quit with her family after the old pastor was fired, one of the prim and proper church mothers, one of the ladies who'd "politely" shamed my mother when she'd left my father, an outspoken non-drinker and non-smoker and non-"adulteress," who'd always worn one of a small selection of formal full-length dresses in church (lighter colors in the summer months only)—what transformed her into this?

Now she's fully into her speech. She alternates between a lilting sing-song-y voice and a screaming roar and a stern sneer and a triumphant exhortation. During the latter points, she stomps her cane on the stage platform for emphasis.

She's saying things that are completely the opposite of, but weirdly the same as, the sort of sermons my ex-pastor gave.

Like him, she's manipulating their emotions—high, then low, then even higher.

Like him, she's telling them they're the superior people of this world, the "chosen ones".

And, like him, she's telling her people that they deserve, and will get, a great reward, in a life much better than this one.

She wails to them about "the great contradiction that isn't really a contradiction. We heighten the sensory feelings in our bodies, so we can escape this bodily realm. To some, that would seem wrong. Many people have been programmed to believe the body is the evil opposite of the spirit and of the mind. But really, the more we use our bodies to resonate, to vibrate, at the higher frequencies of pure ecstasy, the closer we get to the next level of reality, where we depart this dying world, these frail bodies. Becoming beings of pure vibration, pure sensation. That's how the Mayans, the Toltecs, the Atlantians, and so many other past civilizations rose from this realm of existence. They re-tuned themselves to a higher frequency. Like them, we will shed this world of oppression and disease.

"Oh, the remaining inhabitants of the Earth will look for us. But all they'll find are our discarded clothes, our wigs, our false teeth, our pacemakers, our artificial knees, our breast implants, and our jewelry. Our bodies will be gone, to another frequency of existence, where they will emerge perfected.

"Some of the remaining inhabitants of the Earth will ask why we 'were taken' instead of them. They'd been obedient rote followers of an authoritarian religion, an authoritarian politics. They'd repressed themselves, and they'd oppressed others. They'd enslaved themselves to the almighty dollar, while they ruined the planet, the source of all true wealth. Their reward will be to inhabit this world as it becomes ever more uninhabitable.

But we—the freaks, the queers, the woke, the enlightened, the sensuous, the untamed women, the caring men, the non-binaries, the true artists, the lovers, the righteous rebels, the people who give a (S-word) about one another—we are, all of us, whether we all know it yet or not, taking a journey to the next level.

"And that journey, my beloveds, starts tonight."

The DJ running the electronic music feed presses a key on his keyboard, and a sound of a dozen bells pealing comes out of the sound system. Some of the people in the tent raise their voices to cheer; others keep doing the different things they're doing with an extra burst of passion.

I get a sense that a few of these people are looking at me. I'm seated on a bench at the back of the stage. I've been dressed in a bright flowing robe that's tied up in the back. Even weirder, the girl who's come here with me is dressed the same. I still haven't been told what I'm expected to do.

The woman at the front of the stage starts talking again.

"To achieve the final jump, we need to add more people reso-nating the new frequencies from out of different old frequencies, different patterns. More nationalities. More races. More subcul-tures. More genders. More sexualities. As different and disparate as Humanity herself!" More pre-recorded bells. More cheers.

"Within this quest, I offer to you: our new inductee. Someone who may be different from any of you. A person of youth, of limited experience in life. A straight, 'cis,' white male; but, miraculous-ly, not a co-conspirator in the culture of oppression. A person of empathy and compassion. A person of curiosity, of moral purity, if a little timid."

My growing suspicions are confirmed when this woman walks back to take my hand and lead me forward. She reaches in back of me, makes a slight adjustment to the back of my robe, and lets it fall to the stage floor. I hurriedly cover myself with my hands. The people at the benches, women and men alike, cheer and applaud.

I'm so self-conscious, it takes almost a minute before I notice the girl is now standing beside me, now also undressed. I try not to look at her body, which (except for one strange looking tattoo below one breast) is extremely attractive. I also try not to look at her face, which is rapt in some (drug induced?) daze; she's got a glassy-eyed stare and a dangerous looking smile. I thought she'd told me she didn't do drugs any more. Or is she just pretending? I can't tell.

The strangely harmonious blend of noises fades into the back-ground of my mind, affecting me subliminally in some way.

My self-consciousness soon changes to other feelings. I try to think of anything but where I am now. I try to think of stupid, non-sensical, obsessive things to stop the weird emotions and sensations that are taking me over.

Was I drugged again, when I ate from the tailgate picnics outside here? Maybe in the "sugar" I'd put into my coffee?

If I was drugged, it's pretty obvious what one of the drugs was. My hands can no longer hide its effect. I turn my back to the other participants.

But as I do this, the girl catches my eye.

I find I can't look away from her.

My mind becomes a distant spectator, as my body acts on its own.

My body reaches a hand out to the girl. It embraces her, then caresses, then gropes her all over. It then fondles her breasts with one hand and her lower spot with the other.

We kiss on the lips, for the second time.

She touches her hand around my hardened lower front, for the second time.

My powerless mind wonders: So now I know why I've been brought here, why I've been put through everything that's happened in these short few days. But for what purpose?

Is my public mating with the girl really supposed to bring about some sort of alternative Rapture? But that can't possibly happen.

But if I believe, or at least used to believe, in the regular Evangelical notion of the Rapture, what's really so different about this version?

But do I want to help bring the end of the world? No, I don't. But what can I do about it? I can't even control my own body now.

She's fondling and groping me now. Her left hand caresses my lower back, while her right hand caresses my, er, lower front.

My eyes stare into hers, relentlessly.

So relentlessly, I believe I briefly see her slipping me a secret wink.

Suddenly, she pulls her hands away from my lower body and grabs my right hand.

She pulls me along behind her as she turns and runs out of the tent.

The people in the huge tent don't seem to be paying any attention as we flee, both of us still undressed.

She leads me down a curving trail in back of the tent.

After running for I can't think how long, we arrive at another clearing in these woods.

I see "rustic" looking but permanent wood buildings. Long, one-story cabins. A chapel. Another parking lot, under a couple of floodlights, with a couple of yellow buses parked.

We run past a carved, painted wood sign, like the ones in the national forests.

"Camp Philomath."

I've arrived at the place my mother thinks I've already been at.

10.
WHY IS THIS SO CLOSE TO THAT?

The girl is next to me, yelling for me to hurry up.

I've found a suitcase in this sleeping cabin (unlocked, unoccupied) with clothes that more or less fit me. Now I'm looking for a pen and paper to write down the name of the boy whose clothes I'm borrowing, so I can return them to him later. I've been so much in the past few hours; I don't want to also be a thief.

I ask the girl to tell me whose clothes she'd putting on now.

Yes, it's a co-ed sleeping cabin. Under its old pastor, this church wouldn't have allowed teenage girls and boys to inhabit the same building without multiple chaperones. Heck, the old man ordered girls as young as five to either wear skirts in church or not show up.

My wallet, my cell phone—all of them are back at the big tent down the trail, along with my own clothes. We can't go back for them, at least not now.

I don't know if anyone from the tent's searching for us. But the girl doesn't want to take chances. She wants us to get a move on.

I find a pen and paper in another camper's stuff. I write both unwitting clothing donors' names down and put the sheet in a pocket of these pants I've never worn before. They're a bit short and tight for me but they'll have to do.

Now I look for shoes. The ones I find are some gaudy upscale basketball shoes, a little big for me.

I don't even want to think about what I look like. Small jeans, big shoes, a baggy white shirt, a Portland TrailBlazers cap, and a fleece jacket with the sleeves just a little too short.

I barely get the right shoe tied when the girl, having put on a boy's windbreaker, grabs my hand and leads me out.

She's also wearing canvas shoes, a girl's floppy hat, and—oh—a black halter dress. Apparently there was, or will be, a little dress-up dance in this camp. (Why does she look so much more compelling dressed in this than she'd looked completely undressed?) So much for going unnoticed.

Actually, nobody seems to notice us as we skulk around the camp, in search of the spots least illuminated by the floodlights here. We see, but are apparently not seen by, some boys doing joints behind a cabin, some girls doing tobacco cigs between some parked cars, and at least three boy/girl couples in various stages of coupling along darkened trails. We're also not seen by an adult man and woman ferrying supplies in from a van to a modern-looking, long, low building next to the parking lot. We hear noises and see lights from in there. One of the noises is a voice that sounds familiar to me, but not to the girl.

I take the lead in sneaking around to the building's back. The girl really wants us to resume our getaway. But I have to learn what my church youth group, and the youth groups of several other churches from around the region, are doing in there.

I lead her toward a short window. Its outside is near the ground here. Its inside is toward the ceiling of a basement meeting room. I kneel down to look in.

Not only can I see, but also I can hear what's going on inside fairly well, since it's so silent out here.

I see and hear the man of my church's current husband-and-wife pastoral team. The man whose wife had betrayed him, with me.

He's leading the kids through a series of exercises I'd never seen before. He's having everyone stand in facing lines. They all stare for a minute into the eyes of the kid opposite them. Then each line moves one step in a different direction, the kids at the end moving to the end of the other line. Everyone then stares into the eyes of the person who's now opposite him or her. This goes on for a while, apparently until everybody has faced everybody else.

While this is going on, I ask the girl (who's far less interested in this scene than I am) if we'd really prevented the alternative Rapture when we disrupted the orgy ritual back there.

She says probably not. She says the cult's tried to "ascend" from this earthly plane several times before. All that's happened was that they'd had some good sex and some bad hangovers.

If there's really a way to dissolve into another dimension without dying, they're probably doing it wrong, she says. But they won't stop, because the sex is so good, and so is the general "high" of the experience. They're hooked on it, like a drug.

Then the girl tells me she'd been hooked on the cult's rituals herself. It had started when she'd quit meth and hooking at the same time, and was desperate for something else to fill her needs for both sex and excitement.

She looks at me, perhaps to see if I'm embarrassed at her confession. If I am, I don't show it. And I'm not. I'm more emotionally numb than anything else right now.

Still looking in on the spectacle inside, I ask her if she was so into the cult's rituals, how come she'd been alert enough to rescue herself and me.

She says when you've turned tricks for a while, especially with the kind of guys who live around here, you learn to keep a separate part of yourself that's always alert, cynical, and ready to react to anything.

I tell her that's one of the saddest things I've ever heard. Though I'm not looking at her, I can sense her shrugging as she says "whatever."

While we've been having this talk, my pastor inside the meeting room is setting up what he calls "dyads," pairs (mostly boy/girl) sitting across from one another on the floor.

He leads them through what he calls "explorations of the senses."

For Sight: more staring at one another's faces.

For Sound: he blows what he calls an indigenous Australian woodwind instrument at each "dyad." The sound it makes is low and plaintive.

For Smell: he passes out a single flower to each "dyad." He asks each guy to hold it in front of each girl's nose for a full minute, then to reverse it.

For Taste: he passes out a single green grape to each teen. He instructs them to eat it as slowly as possible, one tiny piece at a time, savoring every texture, every solid and liquid aspect, every sensation of the sweet and the tart.

All that's left is Touch. I both want and don't want to know what he's going to do with that.

The girl says she's sure we'll get caught, that the cult people are probably looking for us, that the camp people will find us and then turn us over to the cult people.

I don't really listen to her. I'm rapt by my pastor's actions and his talk.

His voice is soft, smooth, reassuring, yet always in control.

I can tell why my church's deacons picked him and his wife to lead the place, from a national search. He has the charisma to do what the deacons said they wanted—to turn a small Fundamentalist congregation in a suburbanized small town into a big regional mega-church.

When he first came to town, preaching a sunny and optimistic Gospel instead of the fire and brimstone the people there were used to, a lot of the old-time members quit in disgust.

But enough people stuck around, and enough new people joined in, to let the deacons believe they'd made the right choice.

I was at the Sunday service where the co-pastors showed off the plans for the new mega-church building. It'll be big. It'll be modern. It'll have a pro sound and light system and big video flat screens. It'll have an altar area big enough for a seven-piece band and a 20-voice choir. It'll have a restaurant-grade kitchen, and meeting rooms for everything from Weight Watchers to the Soroptimist Club.

And it's all meant to share what the co-pastors call "the good news about the true good life—the life of love and growth spent in family, community, and a personal connection with the Divine." They said at the time that they needed everyone in the church to bring new people in, and to pray and work and give (especially to give) to make this sign of the good Lord's abundance manifest.

I remember that when they showed the big drawing, pasted onto art board, with the new building's exterior view on it, there was no name on the big sign that was pictured to be out in front. The male co-pastor said it was because with a new building, the congregation would adopt a new name. A name more fitting to the new church and its new mission, to exemplify the blessed life in the here and now.

They're still trying to raise that money to build the new church. For now, it's still Calvary Fellowship, in a small fortress of a building with a neon cross on the front outside wall and a purple curtain behind the altar.

And now he's applying the same glib, reassuring soft sell to my teenage youth-group friends.

Well, they're not really that close of friends to me.

We talk before and after our meetings. We sing the songs together; we volunteer at pancake breakfasts together; we play water volleyball at the YMCA together.

But I don't talk to any of them about the more serious sides of whatever I'm going through. I don't tell them how my striving to be a good man has made me feel so alone.

No, only the wife of the husband/wife pastoral team has listened to that. And because she did, I'm here now, on the outside of my own group looking in.

He's having the guys and the girls touch the tips of one another's fingers for almost a minute, then the tips of their noses, then their earlobes, then the napes of their necks, then their clothed tummies, then their...

"Go! Go NOW!"

The girl almost yells in my right ear. She kicks my backside for emphasis.

I almost sprain an ankle as I jump up to a standing position.

She's right.

A man's walking toward us. Slowly.

As a stray light from the building hits his face, I briefly recognize him as the dad of one of the girls in the group. He's a longtime member of my church, from before the new pastors came in.

If he recognizes me, I don't stay to find out.

I follow the girl as she runs into the woods. Her recently acquired reflective jacket (which must have belonged to a girl who jogged or rode a bike) is my only guide into the darkness.

I silently pray that I don't fall into a sudden rabbit hole or stumble on a fallen log or rock or get attacked by a coyote, and that neither does she.

11.
WHY DO I TRUST HER?
WHY DOES SHE TRUST ME?

I awaken for the fourth time tonight.

The rain has come and gone. The skies are clear now. The stars are plentiful now, as such as I can see them.

There's a little patch of sky in my view. Just beyond this carport canopy I'm sleeping under, between some tall, damp evergreen trees.

We're lucky we found this place, wherever it is. And we're lucky there were no fences or burglar alarms or loud dogs to attract attention.

My other recent ordeals were scary or panicky or embarrassing. This one's just plain miserable.

I'm cold. I'm still damp all over, from getting caught in a briefly torrential rain as we were running away.

I'm lying down on a blanket we'd found in the bed of a pickup truck parked here, which in turn is on a concrete floor. I have all my (borrowed) clothes on. I have nothing else with me, and neither does the girl sleeping at my side. She's also still dressed (or rather, underdressed for this weather). She's wrapped the end of the blanket (which smells vaguely like damp animal hair of some kind) over her bare legs.

I desperately need to sleep. I can't. And even if I could, I shouldn't.

We'll have to get back on the road before the sun comes back up.

If I hadn't obeyed her and continued running away from Camp Philomath, I might be sleeping there now, in one of those heated sleeping cabins.

I could have showed up to my male co-pastor, even naked as I was, and been welcomed back like the Prodigal Son. They'd have probably, welcomed the girl as one of their own. They'd have clothed us, fed us, found beds for us, made us feel at home during the rest of the long weekend retreat, and made sure we got home. (Where is her home, anyway? Probably somewhere near that alley where I'd met her.)

I told her his just before we found this place. She said she'd sensed we were still in danger. She was afraid the camp people would turn us over to the cult people.

She asked why the cult's meeting place was right next to the camp. I said it could've just been a matter of coincidence, of two different parties renting different parts of the same property. But even before I finished saying it, I knew that wasn't anything like an airtight alibi. Why was one of the old judgmental church ladies from my church leading the cult's services?

All I know is there's SOMETHING weird going on out there.

But as my female co-pastor sometimes says, live in the Now.

My particular Now happens to be cold, wet, and slightly smelly.

My male co-pastor always exhorts us to take the most positive possible interpretation of whatever situation life gives you, in the reassurance that it's God's will for you to not only survive but thrive, to bloom where you're planted.

In that regard, I tell myself I'm alive. I'm in good health, at least for now. I have a roof of sorts over my head.

I'm with someone who cares about me, or at least seems to.

And, barring getting shot by a vigilante homeowner or run over by an absent-minded truck driver, I'll either be home or on my way home by tomorrow night.

It's still really, really, REALLY cold, though.

I look back at her.

For the second time in my life (also the second time this week), a woman sleeps beside me. This one is sleeping the deep, solid sleep of the just. Her face, as I've mentioned, is a little ragged for someone so young. But her body, as I remember from earlier tonight, is firm and taut.

She's got a toughness that I just don't have. It's undoubtedly because she had to get tough to survive.

Right now I could use some of that toughness. But I sure don't want to have gone through what she must have gone through.

Meth? Ick!

Sex with total strangers? Double ick!

(Though she's really still a stranger to me, and I've sort-of had sex with her. Twice. And, except for the surrounding circumstances, it wasn't bad.)

It may be a superficial vision, but she seems so still, so at peace with these troubling surroundings. Did she ever have to sleep outside before? I mean have to, not like camping out or anything.

I've camped out once. It was one of the last times I was with my father. Was I in middle school yet? I don't think so. He'd decided to have a father-and-son weekend. In retrospect, it was his way to talk to me and get away from my mother at the same time. They were already falling apart as a couple. But I either didn't see it or I chose not to.

Anyway, that campout was perhaps the one father-son bonding thing we had that didn't turn into a disaster. We didn't catch any fish, but we ate well, and we talked well, and he told me campfire stories, and we put up a good tent, and the night was clear and warm, and we cooked up bacon and eggs for breakfast (mother's dietary guidelines be damned), and the Mariners won the game on the car radio on the way home.

For all I know, he's fallen off the face of the earth. If he's ever tried to contact my sister or I, our mother's kept it from us. Weeks, even months, go by and I don't even think about him.

It had been my mother who'd gotten my father, sister and me to start going to Calvary Fellowship, back when it was a fire-and-brimstone independent Fundamentalist church, located in the decaying downtown of a small town that was rapidly turning into a generic suburb. She seemed to think at the time that that church's strict rules of conduct would keep my sister and me in line, and its passionate approach to worship would keep me alert and involved, instead of withdrawing into my own head like I always did (and still do).

Then my father left us, my mother and sister stopped going to church, and I kept going.

They'd given me an "extended family." A stringent, judgmental family, but a family nonetheless.

They tolerated my nerdy aspects, even if their essential ideal of a good Christian boy was still better at sports than I'd ever been.

I kept going, after I started in high school, despite my mother's wavering between indifference and disapproval.

I kept going, after the old pastor was fired, and the new pastors came in with their new vision.

I kept going, after the gossip began to spread about why the old pastor was really fired. (Gossip thrives like wild blackberry bushes in a place like that. That was one of the reasons my mother stopped going.)

I grew up trying to be a Good Person. Not too ambitious, not too selfish, not too crude, not too needy.

And here I am now, about as needy as any middle-class white kid can be.

But just temporarily.

My companion here (it seems weird to think of her as "my friend", let alone "my girlfriend") has been a lot needier for a lot longer. I'm only visiting the sort of unsettled life she's lived in.

I deeply exhale, as I look at her.

Maybe I'm lucky that I haven't had to be tough before now.

No, I know I'm lucky about that.

I've been protected, cradled as it were, by the relative privilege of my life. I've never been really hungry until this weekend. I've never been without a good (if modest) house to live in. I've never needed a dose of illicit drugs just to avoid withdrawal. I've never had to do a lot of the things she's apparently had to do.

Yet she's not been judgmental about me. Or at least she hasn't talked like it. She's been helpful. She's been nice.

Even though she's responsible for us being here now instead of at the camp, it's because she cared about my safety as well as hers. She could have run off herself without even telling me, but she didn't.

All this thinking is finally getting me tired. This is good.

If I don't get up in time to awaken her, she'll get up in time to awaken me. What more could you ask for (well, beyond food and warmth and safety)?

She seems to be asking for something more, silently and unconsciously.

She's not lying still any more. She's rolling around on this smelly blanket, while apparently still sleeping. She's writhing about, restlessly. She's touching, caressing, various areas of her body.

Now she's rolling over again, in my direction.

She's moving right next to me.

I turn on my side, facing away from her.

She becomes still again.

I'm only barely still on the carport's floor. Part of my torso's hanging out beyond the canopy's cover. I don't move.

When we get up, I won't talk to her about any of this.

12.
CAN A ROAD BE EVIL?
CAN A PERSON BE EVIL?

It's sometime Monday morning. By the evening, I'm supposed to be back home.

Right now, it looks like I'll make it, in plenty of time.

Upbeat sports-talk is on the car radio. The voices of boys in men's bodies are yapping about the NFL playoff games coming up next weekend, specifically about the Seahawks' chances to make it back into the Super Bowl. They've really got a lot to say about a single football game that hasn't started yet.

The girl who's been traveling with me is still traveling with me, beside me in the back seat of this car. It's a generic domestic sedan, instead of the generic import sedan in which I'd started this journey.

She'd drifting in and out of sleep on the first couple "legs" of this trip. But she's wide-awake now.

Indeed, it was her legs that got us here. That and her outgoing, take-charge attitude.

Did I think she was a fool for grabbing a little black dress to wear on the road? She was smarter than I thought, turns out.

She got us a ride immediately this morning, just by showing some leg beside the road and making a "please help poor pitiful me" expression. That ride led to another, and then to the one we're in now. It pays to advertise, I guess.

Her visual "presentation" and her persuasiveness got us all the way east from where we'd emerged from the woods, right at a sign advertising the Trysting Tree Golf Course, to the freeway. There, she soon got us a ride north, all the way through Portland. The big city itself, from what I see of it from the freeway, is a blur of nice residential blocks, warehouses, downtown towers, malls, a basketball arena, the river (several times), some beautiful old metal bridges over the river, and so on.

Now we're crossing the big, beautiful, metal freeway bridge into Washington. I don't know what it means for the girl who's stayed by my side all this way; we're heading back away from where I'd last met her. But for me, it's a good sight. It means I'm getting home.

On my first drive south on Saturday morning, I'd followed my instructions perfectly. I avoided the freeway as much as I could, using "surface streets" whenever possible. I was extra careful not to get stopped by any law enforcement, driving well under the local speed limits. I didn't stop for anything except stop signs. If I'd known it would be the last few hours of my old life, before all the craziness, I would have paid more attention to the sights I was driving past. There were some old fashioned main streets with "restored" old hotels and antique marts. There was "the world's largest egg" (just a statue, and not really THAT big a statue at that). There was a plaque honoring something called the Centralia Massacre. Then the bridge into Oregon. From the map on my phone, it was the only bridge across the Columbia for at least 25 miles in either direction.

And now I'm on the Interstate. That, by itself, relieves me. Away from the local weirdness, back on the nationwide grid of reassurance.

I'm on one of "America's great arteries of commerce," as some old educational video I'd seen as a kid had called them. The roads of mainstream middle class America, of people like me. Roads with the great retail and restaurant chains at their sides.

I tell some of this to the girl beside me. She's not buying it.

At first, she goes into a rant about the social, environmental, and other crimes against society inflicted by "the car culture." She talks about these roads as scars on the nation's landscape, destroying small towns and small businesses and the "human scale," along with the big-box chain stores that depend on these roads and the oil companies that destroy the planet to keep these roads running.

It's the first time I've heard her talk about anything beyond herself, the people around her, and our immediate situation. I take this as meaning she's also out of panic mode, like I am, and feels she can now think about less immediate issues.

Then, in a soft enough voice that the folks driving us in the front seat can't year, she talks about a time when she'd been a "lot lizard," turning tricks at truck stops. She says the men, mostly, were lonely and weary and grateful for the chance to touch and (F-word) her body. But one or two of them were really scary, and she didn't have Pseudo-Mom nearby to protect her.

That, she almost whispers to me, is what the freeway means to her.

Whether the people in the front seat heard it or not, they're now turning onto an exit ramp.

There are three of them in the front, and the two of us in the back (plus some boxes and Hefty bags).

They're a girl and two guys. It doesn't seem right calling them a woman and two men, because they talk like boys and a girl in adult bodies, a lot like the dudes on the sports-talk radio. Only these three talk even more informally, like "good old boys" (and girl) but without any accent, at least not that I can tell.

The guy at the wheel is wearing a backwards baseball cap (does anybody still do that anymore?). The cap's front has the slogan FARM BOYS PLOW DEEPER. He screeches in a near-falsetto whenever he really likes something, including things he's hearing on the sports-talk radio.

The girl (really a woman) in the middle of the crowded front seat is equally uninhibited. She's quietly singing/mumbling some hit song I'd never heard before; probably something from a country station. Her dark hair goes just a little bit beyond her shoulders. She's got a denim jacket on.

The other guy has stringy almost-blond hair, and a matching, stringy mustache. He's wearing a purple windbreaker over an embroidered "singing cowboy" type shirt.

From what I can sense of what they've said, they're either two brothers and a sister, or two brothers and a girlfriend. But whose girlfriend is she? She seems to be equally flirty, even "hands-y," to both of them.

Some things they've been talking about don't make much sense. Stuff about how you need more "negative ions" in your water and more "white light" in your food.

Other things they've been talking about make a little more sense. The guy driving told us as soon as they'd let us in their car that they're farm people all right, but they're nothing like the stereotypes city people sometimes have about country people.

The driver said they like to smoke weed.

The woman in the middle says they've got nothing against the gays. The guy with the mustache adds with a snicker, "Especially the gay girls in pornos."

He immediately gives a kiss on the cheek to the woman in the middle, who gives him a brief lip-lock back.

The driver says they believe in a world where all sorts of people can do all sorts of things and it's all for the good.

The woman in the middle says everybody's working for the good of everything. Even the people you think are "bad people" are just doing their part in the big purpose, even if they don't know it.

That sounds like something my co-pastors always say; that you should praise the Lord for everything that comes to you, because it's all in His purpose.

I think about the girl's former creepy customers. I have a hard time thinking of them as not-really-bad. The girl says nothing at this time.

They ask us where we've been and why we want to go north. I don't tell them much about what we've been doing, just that I'm trying to get home from it. The girl tells them only a little bit more—that we'd been at a "gathering;" she implies that it was some sort of neo-hippie get-together, the kind that young people often hitchhike to and from. The three people in the front seat nod; the woman says "right on sister."

They can tell we're tired and we've been through a lot of hassles, especially me. The woman in the middle of the front seat tells us not to worry so much. That just makes you more vulnerable to diseases, she says. She doesn't look back to see the girl next to me giving her a silent raspberry.

The mustache guy says all three of them believe "all the way" in being positive. Everything's going to be OK, he says; and even if it doesn't look that way at the time, it's really all in the Universe's plan. A great big plan, that us little people can only make good guesses about.

The driver adds a little story about himself and his companions. He says he knows he doesn't have to worry about the future. He says his own life course has been destined for prosperity from a long time back. He says the three of them are going to inherit the farm he'd grown up on. They're already convincing his (and the other two people's?) parents about switching the farm to what he calls "sustainable agriculture." (I'm half surprised he can say two long words like that. Maybe I do have stereotypes about rural guys after all.)

He says they're getting away from pesticides and all the chemicals that just hurt the Earth. Just pure methods to make pure foods for pure people. (I bet my mother would like whatever food they grow there.)

I mumble something to the driver about all the unknowns in life. Like the chance of a great big earthquake and tsunami, or just big floods. How do they not worry about things like that?

The woman in the middle answers. She says the farm's located on a plateau, above the local flood plains. If there's a hundred-year flood, or once the global warming really takes hold and the lower lands get swamped, or if that "big one" earthquake sends nearby shore lands into the water for good, they'll be standing tall on their plateau—ready, willing, and able to welcome the refugees from the new wetlands as their new tenants.

I don't tell them their hopes and dreams depend in part on other people's miseries.

The girl tells them she's hungry, but she and I don't have any money.

The woman says not to worry at all. Breakfast is on them.

As she says this, the driver has already pulled over onto an exit ramp.

Within five minutes, we arrive at the front parking lot of a restaurant-bar-whatever called the Kalama Zoo.

13.
IF IT'S SO BAD, WHY IS IT SO GOOD?

It's a comfortable place, the Kalama Zoo. The outside has a big sign saying just EAT, and an abstract metal sculpture of a rooster.

Here on the inside, it's all (real) wood paneling, wood booth seats, and laminated wood tabletops.

Historic signs and framed pictures on the walls here depict Kalama as an old railroad town, complete with its own little "Chinatown" for the Chinese railroad-construction workers. There are old photos of train engines, cars, tracks, and roundhouses.

There's an all-ages dining room up in front here, so I don't have to worry about getting caught underage. I don't believe the girl now sitting across from me is over 21, but I'm not sure. The question hasn't come up; and besides, she doesn't have any ID on her either.

The three people who'd driven us here said we should order everything we want and they'd pay. I tried to just stick to mother-approved stuff like oatmeal and toast with jam. They insisted I eat "real growing-boy food." They ordered it all on my behalf: Hotcakes. Sausage. Bacon. Hash browns. Two eggs. They ordered the same for the girl, but she was able to convince them she's allergic to eggs, so they substituted a giant cinnamon roll. At least I convinced them to let me have grapefruit juice.

And, of course, lots of weak but hot coffee. That arrives first. Within ten minutes, I feel "wired and tired" at the same time.

The taller of the two men in this trio, the one who'd been driving the car that brought us here, suggests that his two companions and him sneak off into the back barroom. He struts back there with his friends? Relatives? Whatever? I see he's got a little tattoo on the back of his hand. I hadn't had the chance to see it while we were in their car. It's a strange abstract black pattern. It looks a lot like the tattoo on the girl's torso.

But before I can get up the nerve to ask her about that, the waitress shows up with lots of hearty, if greasy, food.

The girl dives in. I'm a lot more restrained, at first. Good table manners, my mother taught me at a very young age, are a mark of a true gentleman.

My effort at good table manners fades away pretty quickly. As soon as I get some of the food in me, my body demands more, as quickly as possible.

A greasy fried egg tastes so GOOD to me right now. So do large amounts of butter and syrup on a brown pancake. So does the sweet piece of the fluffy cinnamon roll the girl gives me, with melting frosting. And the bacon: salty and greasy and hot and soft and firm all at once.

I realize that this, not the "healthy" fare my mother feeds me, is real teenage-boy food. So, I figure, are burgers, fries, pizza, chicken wings, burritos. All the things that made fast-food chains and convenience stores such great American institutions.

Then, I think, it's not just the food. A lot of the big stuff in this country, I'm realizing now, is made for teenage boys, or for the teen-age-boy aspects that remain in adult men. Or rather, for teenage boys who are different from me, different from what my mother's tried to make me into.

In a lot of ways, she's succeeded. Either that, or I've just grown up this way anyway.

The fact that I now know I like teenage-boy food doesn't mean that I'm going to start liking a lot of other teenage-boy things. Those stupid, loud superhero movies. Those "gritty," violent games. Rude remarks about girls, rude remarks about "fags," curse words, drinking, drugging, cynically seducing girls and then immediately abandoning them (or at least boasting about it, or at least wishing to do it), and especially strutting around like an "alpha" creep. I still don't care for any of those.

I think maybe that's the reason why I haven't made that many friends in school.

No, that's not it, not completely. I haven't made that many friends; real friends that is, in the church youth group either.

My dining companion doesn't seem to have any second thoughts like this. She just scarfs it all down. She's a girl with a purpose.

Our three benefactors sit back down at our booth. The woman and the taller man have drinks with them that they sit down on the tabletop. They remain seated here for just a few minutes. They then get back up and retreat again to the bar. The taller man gives a wink and a nod to the girl.

Once they're gone, the girl quietly tells me we're supposed to consume these drinks ourselves, preferably while the wait staff isn't looking.

And by "we," she says me. She tells me her sobriety is the most important thing she's got. She says she can get her stuff back from

Pseudo-Mom and her roommates once she's found a new place somewhere. But if she starts drinking and drugging again, it won't be worth an (S-word).

So now I know why she's still riding with me, besides any sense of obligation and/or pity she may feel toward me. She may want to come back to my (and her former) hometown, or possibly to some other promising place along the way.

She gives me the well drink to gulp down quickly. (I don't know what kind it is, but it's colorless). Then she slips me the Bloody Mary (at least I know what THAT is). In both cases, I don't finish them off nearly as quickly as she seems to want me to. If she hates liquor so much, why does she expect me to like it?

Within the next 45 minutes by the big clock above the restaurant's counter area, our three hosts do the same drink-gifting ploy "for" us two more times. Neither the girl nor I dare to decline their "generosity." And we can't leave, because we can't pay.

I DO NOT feel well after drink #5.

I REALLY DO NOT feel well after drink #6.

Unlike the last time I was fed liquor and threw up in public (the girl was there at the time; she should know this about me), I can't do that here at the booth.

I stumble to the men's room, almost knocking over a bus person with a full tray. I have to wait for an available stall for what seems forever. Finally, I do what I must. Then I flush three times and wipe off all the surfaces, to make sure no evidence remains.

I return to the booth. The girl tells me I may have just saved HER life. She says we're now "even."

The three farm people sit back down at the table, even more jovial and high-fiving each other, just long enough to pay the tab. At least they're keeping THAT promise. And they sincerely believe they've done us a favor by sneaking us drinks.

Neither the girl nor I have finished all our food. The woman in the trio chases down a waitress to get us to-go boxes. If the waitress has any clue about my having been fed underage booze, she doesn't show it.

On the way out, we pass the entrance to the bar area. I see a local news blurb on one of the flat screen TVs there. In the closed captions, I read the announcer saying there's some big missing-person story in the Oregon countryside, and that she'll tell all about it at five.

   We all re-enter the trio's car. This time it's the shorter, mustached man who gets behind the wheel. He seems to be the closest-to-sober person among them.

   As he gets behind the wheel, he notices that I'm even queasier than his two compatriots. He announces that he's taking us with them back to the farm. He says they'll make both the girl and I "feel a whole lot better." I'd rather just keep going, even as sick as I am.

14.
WHAT ARE THEY UP TO?
WILL IT HURT?

We've been here about an hour, according to the clock on the kitchen range. Our hosts seem to be in no hurry to help us get back on the road.

This particular "here" is about a quarter of a mile up a private gravel road, off of a narrow, barely-paved road. That, in turn, is a half a mile or so off of a winding country road. That, in turn, is about 10 miles from the restaurant/bar off the freeway where I'd gotten, let's say, unwell.

The house is a little like the house I involuntarily slept in the night before last, except it's got electricity and (thank the Lord) heat. I could recharge my cell phone here, if I still had it.

It looks like it was built in the 1950s, and hasn't been redone much since then. The off-white kitchen, with the round oak dining table I'm sitting at, is as large as the half-paneled, half-wallpapered living room. There's a small hallway with some bedrooms and a small bathroom.

The shelves in the kitchen I'm sitting in have a lot of stuff like protein shake powders, "certified organic" salad dressings, quinoa, and kale.

For three people with these kinds of eating habits, they sure seem to love alcohol. Maybe it's true what my ex-pastor used to say about "the demon rum," that once it gets a hold of you it's almost impossible to get it off of you. I should thank the Lord that I've gotten sick both times I've had it.

They said I could have my pick of anything in here. There are also the leftovers from the restaurant we'd just been to. But I don't want to eat anything now.

All that booze, on a mostly empty stomach, in the morning, in a body (mine) unused to the stuff. Ick.

I still want to get home. But I'm still not quite up to hiking or hitchhiking, especially if I have to do it alone.

I don't see the girl I've been traveling with anywhere near me right now. She walked off with the woman from the three people who'd brought us here a few minutes ago. The woman told the girl that she knew of this great technique to relieve all kinds of stress. She and I have certainly been through a lot of stress. But the girl said she didn't want to. The woman gleefully refused to listen to any of that. She somehow talked the girl into it.

The two guys who also live here are now in the living room of this old style, one-story farmhouse.

The taller one is yapping on a cell phone to somebody. I can't tell what he's saying, except that he's excited about whatever it is.

The shorter guy, the one with the stringy mustache, is even more excited. He's watching some loud superhero movie on a laptop computer. There's no TV set in the room. These people must be like the pompous "alternative" kids in school, the kids who can't stop boasting about how they don't watch TV, but who don't seem to count streaming as "TV".

The guy with the mustache screams his head off in a high tenor; the hero in the movie must have just done something spectacular.

The taller guy waits until that's done, then asks whoever he's talking to on the phone to repeat what they'd just said. He says "Great news!" and puts the phone into his pocket.

Before I can ask him if I can call home on his phone, he walks up to me and slaps me on the back, hard. He says he's just talked to one of his friends, who's the greatest healer he knows. This person, the taller man says, will get me "all aligned" and feeling better in no time.

The girl traveling with me has just re-entered the house, following behind the woman who lives here. The woman kisses each of the two men, on the lips.

The girl looks as bad as I do, but in different ways. I hurt on the inside; she seems to hurt on the outside. She's limping a little, and cradling her left arm with her right arm.

The girl tells me that the woman had "confided" in her; that the woman said she was living out the erotic-romance novel fantasy of her dreams. I wonder if that sort of thing was in the romance novels my mother used to read just after her divorce.

The woman tells me I'm next. I silently gulp.

The woman reaches out a hand to mine, and stands me up. She leads me to an unlit bedroom with closed curtains over the two small windows and a yoga mat on the wood floor. She has me take off my (well, not really MY) shoes but otherwise stay dressed. (At least I get THAT break this time.)

What follows is 20 minutes of what the woman calls "bodywork." Stretching and bending, in turn, each leg, each arm, the fingers of each hand, my neck, and my spine. Cradling my head in her arms, moving it around in one direction and then the other. While she does this, she gives a droning monologue about the eight principles (or is it nine? Ten?) of body/mind balance, of personal harmony, and unleashing the body's natural healing energy. When it's over (thankfully), she lets me lie down on the mat. She perkily asks how much better I feel. I mumble something; I don't tell her I now feel as bad outside as I do inside.

As I walk back (limping a little) into the kitchen, I see a beat-up old red Toyota pickup stopping just outside. A skinny (borderline emaciated) guy pops out of it. He's got blond/gray hair in a pony-tail, with some teeth stained and others missing. He's wearing worn jeans and a red shirt.

When he gets inside and introduces us, he says he too used to hitchhike to "gatherings" in his own younger days. He says he's now 55. That's a minor shock to me; he looks up to a decade older than that.

In a speech pattern accentuated by a lot of "Yup"s and "Huh-huh"s, he says he's going to realign the "polarities" of the girl and me. "Just the free sample session, you know, huh-huh. Not the full one, yup."

Thankfully, it turns out that there's no stretching or bending involved in that.

Just sitting still, while he slowly moves a copper colored device all around (but not on) the bodies of first the girl and then me.

She seems uncomfortable with him. It's as if she thinks he's getting too close to her without her permission; even though his hands and his instrument are at least an inch or two away from her body. For somebody who's apparently had intercourse with total strangers for money several times, she seems strangely disturbed by his non-touching.

He tells the girl that she needs a lot more work to heal the divisions within her spirit and chakra levels, to become more connected with her true self.

But he tells me I've "got the closest thing to a perfect energy flow I've ever seen, yup."

He says he wants to do the whole treatment on me, to put me in full multi-level contact with the Universe. He says he wants to do "Reiki, crystals, light weaving, chakra alignment, the whole bit, huh-huh. You could be famous, yup. You could even become the first perfect being on earth, yup."

Hey, if it can get me out of this place and back on my way home, sure.

I agree, and ask when we can start.

After some drawn-out goodbyes, the girl and I leave the farm-house and approach the cramped quarters of the healer dude's beaten-up pickup.

But just before she opens the passenger's side door, the girl whis-pers to me that she feels something "crazy" about the healer dude. And not a "weird but harmless" crazy, but a "scary" crazy.

I trust her intuition a lot more than I trust his.

But I persuade her to get into the truck anyway.

She gives me a pretty mean look as she climbs in. Even after I whisper to her that we can scram out of the truck once we're on the main road.

She says she knows about scary a lot more than I do. That I've just been a recent visitor to scary-ville but she's lived there.

I cannot argue with her about that, but I get her into the truck anyway.

15.
WHY THE HELL DIDN'T I?

I should have listened to her.

I should have listened to her.

I REALLY should have LISTENED TO HER.

She's the one with the "creepy guy" radar. She gained it because she had to.

She knew there was something, as she put it, "a little weird" about that man.

That man who led to us being in this forsaken place. Stuck, even deeper in Nowhere, Washington.

It's probably still daytime outside. I can't tell from this cement-block room with no windows. There's a rolling-steel-slat garage door; airtight (or at least light-tight) and locked. There's a heavy steel door leading to another room. The energy healer (and, it turns out, part-time muscle-car mechanic) is on the other side of the door, preparing who-knows what to do to me and maybe to the girl with me as well.

We're sitting on a workbench. Well, really she's sitting up and I'm lying down, still a little queasy and a lot weary. She's got so much more stamina than I've got.

This place is even further from the main county road than the previous place we'd been at.

Mounted on the walls are metal signs (some maybe authentic; others obviously newer fakes) advertising long-ago gas brands: Signal, Carter, Enco, Richfield, Gilmore, American, Flying A.

There are three cars in this large, poorly lit garage space: A midget race car with the engine removed. A black '60s muscle car on blocks. The outer shell of a 1930s Lincoln convertible, with the seats, steering column, and other parts scattered next to it.

I swear I remember the muscle car from somewhere.

Nah, it couldn't be that. It couldn't be HIM.

One of my sister's old one-to-five-night stands. The one who had umpteen broken-down cars parked in various places. I'd never met him, only heard what my sister had said about him, how at first he'd seemed like an older guy who still had the spirit and ambitions of a younger guy, and how she split once she realized his talk about being on the verge of big success always was, and would always be, just talk.

I don't remember her saying if he was into weird healing regimens. I think she might have said something about him having a "crystal obsession," but I though she meant the drug. Yes, she had that bad a taste in boyfriends, and hasn't gotten much better since.

I realize I've been traveling with this girl for two days and haven't asked her how much she remembers about my, and her former, hometown. I've either been too obsessed with my own fate, or too frozen in fear and panic, or both.

I'm trying to remember her as she was. A little older than my older sister. Already into the "wild life" or as close to it as you could get in the subdivisions. Parents who didn't know what to do with her, who kept praying in our church for her safety. Since my own mother had stopped going to church, they were sort of substitute parents to me when I was at services.

Then the pastor became the ex-pastor. Her parents were among the families who dropped out of Calvary Fellowship right after. I didn't see them, or her, again. Until two days ago.

She's still sitting up and I'm still lying down when I ask her about her younger days.

She says I don't want to know.

I say I do.

She starts in with a "condensed, clean version" of the story.

She was 14. I would have been 9 or so.

She says up to that time she'd been a loudmouthed girl, a "precocious" girl as her parents had put it, a girl who liked to exchange dirty jokes with the other girls and share an occasional joint out behind the Fred Meyer store, but nothing more than that. She still went to church dutifully with her parents, only occasionally making faces during the sermons.

The then-pastor had contrived some excuse to keep her in the building after the Wednesday afternoon Bible study. He offered her a tour of the parts of the church building most people didn't get to see. He took her to the organ pipe room behind the altar stage. He took her to the dressing room for brides and bridesmaids. He took her to the old "parsonage" apartment in the half-basement. There, on an overstuffed sofa in the gaudy gold color he loved so much, he sat her down and told her he'd taken her aside because he could tell the devil was within her. He took her by the hand, looked her straight in the eye, and said the only way to push the devil out was....

I tell her she doesn't have to go into the gruesome details if they're too disturbing for her.

She thanks me, but says those emotional scars were bled dry long ago. I don't tell her that's a mixed metaphor.

She says she'd told her parents. They told her she'd made it all up, and was a bad girl for having done so.

That, she says, is when she stopped listening to them, or any other authority figures, and started down the life path that led to the alley where we'd re-met.

A year later, she says, the board of deacons finally heard enough stories from enough people they trusted to fire the pastor from the church his own parents had founded. Because it was an independent church with no denomination, he couldn't simply be transferred to another post in another town. The deacons made up a story about wanting to take the church into "new growth areas" or some such (S-word). To cover up any impending scandal, they "persuaded" some of the old man's most faithful followers to also leave.

She says she's not in contact with what she calls her "birth parents," or anyone else from the old town, at least not too much. But she says she'd learned that the old reverend had had a lot of the congregation's women, and girls, and boys.

I immediately think: if he'd still been there when I was a year or two older...

The healer dude opens the big metal door and says he's finally all set up and ready to "take a reading" on me, "yup."

He leads us back into the front room of this place, apparently an old mom-and-pop store and gas station. The girl passes him with a stern, "Don't you DARE get any closer to me" stare.

The former grocery-store room still has a couple of old signs for Double Cola and Sunbeam Bread. But the rest of the decor is all meditative, with crystals and night-sky posters.

This room has windows to the outside. It's still light out.

Along a counter, he's set up what look like they could be props in a high school theater production of "Frankenstein."

He has me drink a glass of water from a tap with a weird filter device on it. Just before he gives me the glass, he brings out a dropper-bottle of something colorless and squeezes exactly three drops of it into the glass. He tells me some weird name for it that I immediately forget. He says it will free up any frozen ions in my system. I drink it. A slight metallic taste, but very slight. He offers a glass to the girl who's with me; she silently refuses it.

He has me take my shoes off and lie down, face up, on a folding massage table.

He then walks around the room to dim the lights and start up an MP3 of tuneless bass-synth vibration sounds.

He returns to me with what he calls a "light energy chakra-healing wand." It's a different model than the one he'd used on me back at the farmhouse. He said that one was for diagnosing. This one's for "treatment." It has a white, iPod-like thing on its back end. He shows me how the little screen on the device shows him what to do where.

He places the wand on, or just above, most of my clothed body. I don't see what's on his little screen, but I can hear it beep and buzz at odd intervals.

He has me turn my body face down on the table. He resumes getting his "readings."

I can't see what he's doing now, but I hear him put that device down, and then start up another one.

It turns out to be two other devices, one in each hand. He touches me with both things at once. They make a weird buzzing sound. I feel my body changing in response.

By the time he has me turn over again, keeping my eyes closed, I'm feeling both totally calm and totally disoriented at once.

I fall into a trance, but a different kind of trance than the one before at the tent meeting. The synth ambient "music" track and the rising and lowering buzz of his handheld devices put me at ease, even as I start to feel really weird in a way I never have.

I feel myself not passing out, but passing "through." My clothes (well, they're not really mine) feel like they're about to fall off of my dissolving physical body.

I open my eyes and look at my left hand. It seems to not even be there. I blink and it's there again. I blink again and it's not. I ought to be scared as all hell, but instead I'm almost completely relaxed.

I hear the Healer Dude putting the devices down onto the counter. I hear him walking around. I don't have the energy to raise my head to look.

Thankfully, the girl is there to yell at the dude to stop the procedure. When he doesn't, I hear her run to the far wall. She gets down on her knees. She unplugs the power strip that all his devices are connected to; I can tell because they all go silent at once, even the music player.

She raises me up by my shoulders. She gives me two sharp slaps in the face.

I open my eyes for good. I shake myself around. I look down at myself. I'm still here. I'm still me.

So the cane lady's "sermon" at the tent meeting, about ascending to a higher frequency—it might have been true, in a way.

The healer dude paces around, panicky. He says he's so, so sorry. He says he'd never seen anyone respond so "effectively" to the treatments. He says he doesn't know what to do.

The girl tells him what to do, fiercely.

She tells him we won't sue the (D-word) off of him ONLY if he drives us home.

He asks where to. She tells him. Yes, at least two hours away, maybe three. And starting now.

He complains that his pickup, the only working vehicle he's got, isn't in that great of shape. He doesn't know if it can go that far in one drive without breaking down.

She says we'll take that risk.

She helps me sit up and get my (well, not really my) shoes back on.

We're on the road again.

16.
IF WE DON'T STAY HERE, WHERE DO WE GO?

Now we're REALLY on the road again. On foot, even.

It's after dark, and clouding up again.

We're just off the freeway.

The exit sign said GRAND MOUND. Yes, the girl with me made a dirty joke about the name. She rubbed her cleavage in the black dress against my face as she said it.

She was sitting on my lap at the time, as she had this whole ride. I presume it was to avoid any risk of touching the dude driving the pickup.

The Healer Dude's beater pickup had managed to run for about an hour before it started making funny noises, then serious noises. He'd barely gotten it off of the freeway and onto a "surface street" before it stopped altogether.

He got out and started to tinker under the hood, with tools from a toolbox he kept in the club-cab area behind the seat.

We got out too.

He gave us some money to spend at one of the many fast-food outlets near the exit.

The girl saw a sign across the street for something called MARI-JUANA MART and said she wished she could go there instead, if it wasn't for this (F-word) precarious sobriety of hers.

We got what looked like the most filling fare we could get for the money. Yep, more convenience store microwave burritos and snack foods. I'm starting to like these things. They're warm. They're hearty. They're predictable.

We've now walked back to the pickup.

The eating and the walking have helped me to feel stronger, more alert, more "in my skin" as it were.

He's still trying to figure out what's wrong with the truck now. There are two gas stations back where we'd been by the fast-food places. But he says he wants to do this himself; that he can do it himself; that he's done it himself a half dozen times before. I don't say he might not have needed to do it the last five times if he'd had someone fix it the first time that knew how.

He doesn't want any of our food. Too processed, too gluten-y. I ask him what else he can't eat. He gives a really long list: wheat, dairy, complex carbs, "bad fats," red meat, anything microwaved, anything with hormones, anything with fructose, anything "genetically modified," etc.

Now I know how he stays so skinny. He can't eat anything. At least my mother's idea of healthy food includes, you know, food.

The girl insists he let us use his phone. He warns us it's on a pay as you go plan and it's almost out of minutes. I call my mother. No answer. I call my sister. I'm halfway through leaving a message when the phone dies. At least she'll know I'm alive somewhere, after the bus from the church camp rolls into town with me not on it. That should be in maybe an hour or two. The bus has probably passed this spot on the freeway by now. We couldn't have stopped it anyway.

The girl really wants us to get going on our own. She says if he's as good at fixing his truck as he is at fixing humans, he'll be here a long time.

We tell him we'll try to get a ride up on the old Highway 99.

He warns us it probably won't work. People don't stop for hitchhikers much around here, he says. Too afraid of carjackers.

We leave anyway, mainly because she doesn't trust the dude with her safety or mine.

We walk over the overpass. I pause in the middle to look down on the busy freeway. There's so much action and movement down there, and almost none on the nearby surface streets. All those cars. All going somewhere. All carrying humans. And semis, tanker trucks, and vans. And RVs and travel trailers, carrying weekend vacationers back to their homes. And a few motorcycles. The floodlit lanes, running smoothly and speedily. Northbound and southbound.

To her it was, and still is, a scary place. A dangerous place. A place where people can do bad things and then just drive off.

To me, not too many hours ago, it seemed like an inviting place, a place of relative safety, a place of the familiar routines of regular American life.

Now, I'm not so sure. It's more like a lonely place, a place of dull rote activity. A place where only two things happen: everything works and people and things get where they're going, or there's an accident and they don't.

We resume walking across the overpass.

We stop to stand at a spot just short of the northbound on-ramp.

She has us stand under a floodlight in front of the FREEWAY ENTRANCE sign. She tries different stances and poses, to show off her legs and her (not really "her") black dress.

Few vehicles pass us. None stop.

We get back to talking.

I ask her if she'd ever been a friend with my older sister, who's still a year or two younger than she is.

At first, she says she doesn't remember her.

I tell her a few more defining characteristics that applied to my sister back when I was 8 and she was 11 (and the girl I'm telling this to would have been 13 or 14).

Eventually, she does find a few memories of my sister. She remembers her as having been a wild girl just like she was. Sneaking smokes and drinks and joints. Talking trash whenever the grownups weren't around. Learning all the "explicit lyrics" hiphop tracks. Finding ways around the anti-porn filters on their home computers.

Now, the girl adds, she doesn't remember my sister having specifically done any of those things. They were just some of the activities that went along with the personality type.

She says Fundamentalist churches were great at breeding wild girls. In a place where the definition of a nonconformist was so wide and at least seemed to be so fun, and the definition of being a conformist was so narrow and known to be boring as (F-word), the idea of being a rebel was just SO appealing.

Especially when conformity meant you had to let the creepy ancient minister feel you up with his liver-spotted hands when nobody was looking.

My past just keeps getting worse, just like my present.

Yes, I was just a little boy at the time. And an introverted, loner little boy at that.

But damn it, I should have known something was wrong. I should have been able to do something about it. I should have done something about it.

But what COULD I have done?

I just realize: Have I ever used words like "damn" or "hell", even in my thoughts, before this weekend?

After about a minute of my awkwardly not saying anything to the girl, I'm thankfully interrupted when a vehicle slows down and stops in front of us.

It's what my sister would call a "big ass" SUV. Black paint; black tires; black bumpers. It would probably have had black license plates if this state issued them.

The Healer Dude's in the back seat; he's waving at us, to get us to approach the thing.

The man driving it is a big guy. About twice the girth of the Healer Dude. He looks like he could eat the Healer Dude as a late night snack (but would probably find him too tough and stringy). His hair and beard and bushy eyebrows are as black as his leather jacket and all the rest of his clothes are. Only his face and hands are pale.

The woman beside the driver looks like a tribal member. Short, with wide shoulders. A roundish, still face, with prominent cheeks and eyebrows. Cute, in an "I don't know I'm cute, but I really do" sort of way. (I realize that doesn't make any sense.) She's all in denim; dressed warm for this time of year. She smiles at us, while the man beside her just gives off a steely glare.

I've never seen them before, but the girl with me tells me she thinks she might have, somewhere, at least one of them.

The Healer Dude lowers his right rear window. Again, he motions for us to approach him. I lead; the girl I'm with still seems to not trust him.

The dude tells us he'd gotten just enough power on his phone to call them. They live near here. The woman is his ex girlfriend, and the man is the guy she'd left him for. But they're all good friends these days, even though (or because) he now lives a couple of counties south of them.

The tribeswoman (if that's what she is) gets out of the SUV. She says something to the Healer Dude. Something short and not too emotional. The Healer Dude gets out. They trade places: she gets in the back seat and he gets in the front. It's as if the Tribeswoman (if that's what she is) knows that the girl doesn't want to sit next to the dude.

The (presumed) tribeswoman motions to the girl with a big "get your body over here" arm gesture. The girl approaches her. Across the right-rear door, the tribeswoman tells the girl to get in, that she can trust her, that everything's going to be fine.

It seems to work at defusing the girl's creepy-guy radar. Either that, or she doesn't want to spend more hours standing out here in just a short dress and a jacket.

She climbs into the back seat. I follow her in. I close the door.

I can barely introduce myself to the tribeswoman before her man cranks up the sound system in the SUV. Oldies gangsta rap, with the bass turned up to permanent-ear-damage levels.

Before I can try to open the door, we're on the move. Away from the freeway.

In the front seat, the Healer Dude just nods and goes "Yup."

The driver guns it, slowing down only when he sees a police car in the distance. He's got a headset on, probably connected to a cell phone, and yaps into it. How he can hear what he's saying, let alone what the other person on the line's saying, is a mystery.

The tribeswoman just smiles and blissfully moves in her seat to the music.

The girl and I look at one another. It's hard to tell who's more scared, since we're both trying to hide it.

17.
CAN I EVEN SAVE MYSELF?
SHOULD I?

From the outside, this place looked like a regular exurban McMansion. A place of standard-issue opulence, of cookie-cutter luxury, at the end of a long driveway, atop a small hill. A black import convertible was parked outside a three-car garage. The house itself was bathed in lights, fully visible from the road below. It had a pseudo Early American look, with white shingled walls and blue trim on the windows. Strings of Christmas lights were turned off but still installed along the exterior corners and the sloped roof.

Inside, it's somewhat tackier.

Gaudy, gold-painted, fake "antique" furniture. A '70s style shag carpet, with what looks like cigarette burns in a couple of places. Two black velvet paintings of naked Hawaiian princesses. A flat-screen TV along, and almost the size of, one wall. A gas fake-fire in a fake-boulder-lined fireplace. A hideous, gigantic, lime-green floor lamp.

I hadn't noticed, when I was riding in the SUV of the couple who lives here, just how big the man is. At least six-foot-two, with huge arms and a huge beer belly. He's plopped himself down in a big black La-Z-Boy. He looks like he could just sink into there and never re-emerge. He's unzipped his leather jacket but kept it on, over a black T-shirt with an image of a snarling bulldog. He's said barely 10 words since we entered the place.

The tribeswoman has done all the work of making the girl, the Healer Dude, and I to "feel right at home," as she put it. She got a whiskey bottle with shot glasses for her man and herself, a hard cider for the Healer Dude, and (at our insistence) just bottles of Sparkling Ice for the girl and me. The whiskey and glasses came from a glass-doored wood cabinet here in the living room; the rest she got from your basic McMansion kitchen, all stainless steel with a countertop "island" in the middle, on the other side of an open archway from this room.

She's now seated in a fake-antique chair, next to the fake-antique sofa where the rest of us sit.

The big man has used his big remote control unit to pipe in some music. Thankfully, it wasn't loud gangsta rap this time, but the Music Choice 'Smooth Jazz" cable channel.

The tribeswoman did most of the talking.

She asked Healer Dude what he'd been up to lately. He said he had one new patient (not paying yet). He said he'd healed the back pain she'd suffered from for years, just with two treatments. He said he had four "project" cars, one of which was almost ready. The tribeswoman noted that he'd said the same thing about the same car when they'd last talked, about a year ago.

When the Healer Dude asked the tribeswoman what she and her husband were up to, she said, "Oh, the usual." Their business was going well. Tiny house kits and blueprints, guidebooks for living "off the grid." Canning supplies. No matter who wins elections, she says the market for what she calls "survival gear" just keeps rising.

The girl who's traveling with me says something about how the couple's living in a huge house with cable TV and everything, by convincing other people to live in shacks without electricity. The tribeswoman grins and says "Yeah, that's about it."

The tribeswoman asks about me, making some semi-caustic "joke" about me being so quiet and shy. I mumble something about being a little tired and just wanting to get home, up north a ways, which was where we were going before the healer's truck broke down. She makes a faked-insulted remark about what; this place isn't good enough for me? I turn my head in faked embarrassment.

Then she stands and offers us a tour of the house.

The healer, the girl, and I follow her, first into the kitchen. The big man in the La-Z-Boy stays behind. He gets his cell phone from out of his jacket pocket and puts his headset back on.

The rest of the house is about the same as the living room. In the kitchen, there's a baby-crib area with a blanket at its bottom that reeks of dog hair. She tells us they've got four dogs, which are sleeping in their "outside house" right now.

She has us look into, but not enter, a "study" room. I only get to glance for a second at the books on the shelves, with titles that talk about "the coming tribulation," "surviving the fall of America," and making your own beer.

I'm getting my own "creepy guy radar" starting to act up here. I try to tell myself that these people aren't crazies themselves; they're just making money selling to crazies.

The tribeswoman leads us up some wide stairs to the second floor.

The master bathroom has a large slate-floored shower and a large tub with a built-in Jacuzzi.

The master bedroom has a walk-in closet, with a lot more women's than men's clothes. The woman says her husband is "a creature of habit," and not "a flashy dresser by any means. But I love him." She gives a "just between us dames" wink to the girl, implying what? That the couple living here has a good sex life? I don't want to even think about that right now.

Then I turn to look at the big bed frame.

The front and side bed boards are made of a dark-stained wood. And they have relief carvings of old shooting rifles.

In what the woman calls her husband's "den" (a wood-paneled home office room), more old guns are on display in the form of framed paintings.

Her own "dressing room," on the other side of the walk-in closet, is all done in native arts and crafts.

We re-descend the stairs and enter the garage. There's a large travel trailer, and shipping boxes, and supplies for their online sales business. There are catalogs and stickers with a logo of a stern-faced man in camouflage holding up a big gun, against a backdrop of the smoking ruins of a city.

Our hostess makes no remarks about any of this. But she does say she's got a "big surprise" in store for us.

She presses a panel on the garage wall. A portion of the wood floor slides back, revealing narrow stairs leading downward. We can only descend one at a time: first our hostess, then the Healer Dude, then me, then the girl.

Down here, there's a room walled by plain white sheetrock and lit by naked white light bulbs. The ceiling is short. An unfinished-wood door leads into a larger room. It's a shooting range.

Now I'm really creeped out. I tell our hostess it's been fun and everything, but I really want to get back on the road. The Healer Dude says likewise.

Our hostess, as perky as ever, says "Sure."

She leads us back up the narrow stairs.

It's not until I'm all the way up that I notice the girl isn't behind me.

I look down and see she's still at the bottom of the stairs. The big man is holding her by the arm. Before I can see the expression on her face, the floor panel slides shut.

The woman is still bearing her hostess-with-the-mostest smile. "Of course I'll drive you home. I understand it's like two hours away from here, right? That'll be perfect. Oh, by the way: If you try to come back here, well I told you about the dogs, right? But I don't think I told you about the laser alarms around the perimeter, or the gun sights we've got from the top floor windows. Besides, by the time it takes you to get back here, your friend the street whore, and yes we could tell that's what she was, why she'll be off on her way to a terrific new life. No pimps, no johns, no streets."

I stand there, mouth open.

"Your hooker friend will now be a mail order bride! Well, really an e-mail order bride. Oh, she'll have a GOOD home in the militia compound, safe behind armed sentry lines! Well, there IS the little matter that there's no electricity there, or running water. Or cell service. But hey, roughing it can be FUN, right? Now, shall we go? I'd like to get going, and so does my 'housewife's helper.'"

She opens her coat to discreetly show off her "housewife's helper." A small, sleek handgun, on a small, discreet holster belt.

We're (the Healer Dude and I, that is) on the road again.

18.
DO I REALLY HAVE ANY CHOICE?

And now we're off the road again. Well, off the freeway.

Among the things I can praise my Lord God for these recent days, one of them can surely be the lousy gas mileage of ridiculously large SUVs.

We're stopped at a brightly lit modern gas station, an island of garish light amid the darkness of this cloudy but (so far) dry night.

This stoppage has also stopped, for now, my grilling/inquisition of the tribeswoman driving the Healer Dude and myself, a woman who has also turned out to be a kidnapper, pimp, and "human trafficker." Along with gun running and who knows what other sins.

Though I have to admit that what I've been doing with her hasn't really been heavy "grilling." I've mumbled a few questions to her, and she's answered, in a perky and proud manner.

(The Healer Dude, in the SUV with her and me, has said even less than I have on this trip. Nothing at all, in fact. He's just cowering in the back seat, trying hard to avoid getting into any deeper trouble than he and I are already in.)

For a criminal, she's sure eager to talk about what she does, with no sense of guilt or apology at all.

Maybe she's like what my male co-pastor said in a message about the differences between loud superhero movies and the real world. In the real world, he said, evil people don't always come right out and say, "I'm evil." Instead, they often say, "I'm so good, so totally and completely good, that I can do evil things and it's OK." He used some fancy term for the syndrome. He called it "moral relativism" or "relativity" or something like that.

But anyway:

I managed to ask the woman driving this SUV, who looks like she's presumably a tribeswoman from one of the local native nations around here, why she and her (presumably white) husband took the girl who'd been traveling with me as a prisoner, to be sold and shipped off to be an "e-mail order bride" at some survivalist militia camp somewhere out in the far countryside, probably in another state. (Wait: that would be interstate trafficking, probably another crime she and her husband are into.)

The woman went into a smiling, self-serving speech about the many different things she and her husband do for money. I, of course, have no idea whether she was telling the truth about all, or any, of it.

She said they were firm believers in the American dream, the dream of what she called "liberty," the dream of making the most of yourself with the least interference from governments and go-gooders, people she dismissed as "social justice crusaders" as if that were a bad thing to be.

"I bet I know what you're gonna ask next. And the answer is, Hell yes!" She said she knew that some of the people to whom they sold "goods and services" were what she called "white nationalists." But then she said that Native Americans were the one minority group that white nationalists liked, admired. "To people like them, people like me represent the valiant warriors, the noble holders of ancient wisdom, and all that nonsense. Profitable nonsense for me, mind you."

She added that she's gotten more money from her racist clientele than she ever did from the Federal government, which still won't even legally recognize that her own particular Indian tribe exists.

No, she said, the way to success for people like her was to stop depending on "big government," and to start "doing things for us. Freedom to the individual ought to be the chief value of any society."

I tried to butt in with a few quiet words about how come her ideas of "liberty" and "freedom" seemed to include the "freedom" to take away the girl's freedom.

She said it was "a dog eat dog, every woman for herself, world out there. Besides, we both know that even if your hooker friend wanted to stop turning tricks and stop doing meth or crack or whatever, it wouldn't last. It never does for those people. She'd be back on her back in a week, two most.

"But this way, she'll be part of an extended family.

"Just think of it: She will be in a tightly knit community, among people who'll care for her, and she'll learn to care for. She'll have a husband who keeps her sober and keeps her protected. She'll have kids who'll grow up learning to take care of themselves for their own sake. And, if those suckers ever get their (S-word) together and actually carry out the 'second amendment revolution' they're always hyping it up about, this onetime street crack whore will be one of the 'triumphant vanguard' of the 'new American order.'

"And before all that, she'll have little me to be with her. To prepare her for her journey of a lifetime, to 'persuade' her that this is the best thing that could ever happen to a loser like her.

"So you don't have to worry your cute boyish blonde head any more about that little piece of white trash snatch you got yourself all hung up on. I'm gonna get you back to your sweet little home in the sweet little suburbs; which, by the way, will be the second places to get destroyed, right after the big cities, when the big 'new civil war' comes. You just go back to your homecomings and prom nights and PTA bake sales and knocking up sweet young girls in the back seats of your Volvos."

It was just after that that the FUEL LOW sign started to flash on the big fancy dashboard of this big SUV. She got off at the nearest exit, and pulled into the nearest station.

She's gotten outside the vehicle now.

Yes, I'm definitely back in Washington, a state where you DO pump your own gas.

Only now does the Healer Dude say anything.

He says that back when he'd been seeing the woman, she hadn't been that selfish or that, well…

I say, "That criminal?"

He says that's one way to put it. He says she'd certainly been an ambitious woman, a woman who wanted desperately to create a better life for herself, and a woman who didn't really give much thought to who she burned or cheated on her way up in life. He says he's glad now that she'd left him, even though at the time it was due to some other reason, to his own being too depressed and introverted for her tastes.

He says he knows the woman won't let him out of the vehicle before she's taken me home, and that that's almost two more hours of driving time away. He says he wishes he could just sneak out and get back to the broken down pickup he'd abandoned back at the Grand Mound exit.

I remind him that she's right outside the vehicle, with a gun.

No, it would be better if we could just drive off with her still outside, if she'd somehow left the key in—

Then I realize, and then he realizes, that she DID leave the key in.

She puts the gas cap back on. Before she's done putting the hose back onto its receptacle on the pumps, I jump into the driver's seat.

I've tried to be a cautious driver, during my first year of having a license. But this time I rev off as fast as I can. I don't even notice whether she's cussing me out back there at the station.

I can keep going further away from here, and will be safer if I do.

I CAN go home, now that Healer Dude and I have full control of the SUV.

The Healer Dude even suggests that I do just that—that I drop him off at the Grand Mound exit, and then head straight for my home. He says I should abandon the SUV as close to the freeway as possible, and then walk the rest of the way home.

He gives me some excuse about taking care of one's own self before trying to save the world.

I won't have it.

For once, I'm going to be what my female co-pastor calls "active for good."

I tell the dude we're getting the girl back. We. He's GOING to help me do it. I have no other choice, and neither does he. "End of discussion."

Not that he's been that talkative anyway.

19.
I'M DOING THIS, BUT HOW?

I realize something now.

I realize I should have paid more attention when I was first driven up this road. And the Healer Dude (still in the back seat of this monster SUV) should have, too.

I know I can't expect the big house on the hill to be lit up like it was when we first went there.

I know I can't expect a warm welcome once I find it and get there. Except from the big bulldogs they said they've got there. And maybe from the gun lookouts they said they've got there. And maybe from some henchmen who might have already been in the house, or might have quickly shown up there when the lady of the house called up, which she undoubtedly did when we ran off without her and left her with the gas bill.

This is easily the most dangerous thing I've ever done.

At least it's the most dangerous thing I've ever done by choice.

As if I had a choice, which I really didn't.

Because when the girl said we were "even" when I drank her drinks for her at the Kalama Zoo, we weren't.

I owe my life, and maybe the survival of the world as we know it, to her.

That's the kind of debt you don't shirk on.

At least it's not the kind of debt I'd shirk on.

At least not now.

If I'd remembered the address (if I'd even seen it; did I?), I could have the navigation system tell us the way.

But then again, I remember the female co-pastor telling me on the first day of this misadventure not to use the navigation in THAT car. She'd said she didn't know if "the authorities" could trace the signals from those things, but she didn't want to risk it.

Now I'm thinking whether the tribeswoman and her big husband could trace any navigation signals from this thing. Could it happen?

But does it matter? They should know I'm going to try to get the girl out of there. Even though they've got a lot of guns and neither the dude nor I even has a currently working cell phone.

The dude in the back seat is as silent in the face of danger as I used to be, and not that long ago. I was, as he is, only concerned about my own survival.

The tribeswoman and her big husband are only concerned about their own survival. That's their excuse for selling guns and crap, at probably highly inflated profits, to those guys out in rural Idaho or Montana or whatever. The guys who call themselves "survivalists." Guys who think—no, absolutely believe—they're going to overthrow the U.S. government, the holders of the biggest military arsenal in the history of the world, with handguns and hunting rifles.

And this couple wants to make the girl I've been traveling with (can I call her "my girl"? Probably not; even though we've had sortof-sex twice) into one of the survival-cult people?

To even make her WANT to become one of the survival people?

I.

Don't.

Think.

So.

Now, if I only knew how to get there.

And what to do when I do get there.

I think I'm on the right road now. I think I remember its particular curves, its particular hillsides on one side.

I just have to slow down, and make sure I choose the correct long uphill driveway.

The Healer Dude in the back seat starts to complain, non-verbally. He's growling and coughing and fidgeting in his seat (I can hear the vinyl seat cover squeaking).

If I were a more cynical person than I am (or as cynical a person as he currently wants me to be), I could tell him that for someone who claims to be this big energy and spiritual healer, he sounds really sick.

But I don't.

I don't turn around to look at him, but I start to wonder. What if he really is sick? At least from the stress of thinking about what I'm about to make him do?

This gives me my first idea of how I'm going to do this.

I tell him my plan.

I'll let him stay in the SUV, to keep it idled, while I investigate inside the big hillside McMansion house.

When the girl and I come out, he is to let us in and then get us the hell out of here.

And until that happens, he's not supposed to open the SUV's doors to anybody else.

That's all he has to do.

I ask him to climb into the front seat. He does.

He looks even paler and thinner than when I'd first seen him, a few hours and a couple of worlds ago.

His hands are shaking a bit. More than a bit, really.

His gray/blonde hair seems to have become gray/white. But that could just be the lighting conditions in here.

I ask him if he's really ready, and really willing, to do this.

He gulps a little and says "Yup."

We're on it, as they say in those loud superhero movies.

I speak out a prayer for the Lord to protect the girl, the healer dude, and me, and to show me the way.

Soon, I find what's almost certainly the darkened driveway up the hill to the darkened McMansion.

When I steer the SUV onto the driveway, no lights come on. No alarm sounds.

When I get the SUV to the front of the big house, no lights come on there either. I hear no gunfire or anything else. Not even any yapping from the big bulldogs, which the wife said were there but I didn't actually see.

It's been long enough I'd left here that they could have split. Did they? There's only one way to find out.

I instruct the Healer Dude, again, to get into the driver's seat of the SUV and to stay here. He doesn't seem relieved that we haven't faced any trouble yet. He's obviously still scared as hell of what might happen in the next few moments. I tell him it's all going to be fine, that the Lord Jesus is on our side. He doesn't seem at all reassured by what I say. Not at all.

I'm a little, no a lot, hesitant myself as I open the SUV door and climb down from its heights to the ground-stone driveway.

It takes me a second to notice that the black convertible that had been in this driveway is gone now. I vaguely see the outline of some other vehicle in the distance, in the dark. I don't think about it now. I have other obsessions.

I don't have any clue whatsoever about where to go, what door to try first. I wait for an inspiration from the Lord.

Whether it's from Him or from my own head, I get the idea to just try to break in from the front door.

It's not locked.

I open the big, heavy front door.

I look into the living room. I see nobody. The dimmer lights are down low.

I look for the dimmer switch and turn it up.

The male pimp (which is what I just now decide he should be called), as far as I can tell, is gone.

The female pimp (the wife, the tribeswoman, my former driver, my former hostess), as far as I can tell, has not returned.

In the back of the room, on the gold-painted, fake-antique sofa, the Girl sits. She's apparently unharmed. She's bearing a very "neutral" expression on her face.

The black dress she'd been wearing is now strewn across the floor.

And somebody else is with her.

20.
WHERE DO WE GO FROM HERE?
AND WHEN DO WE GO?

"We've all been waiting for you, kid. What took you so long?"

It's the woman that the Girl calls her "Pseudo-Mom," her female former pimp and I'm not sure what else.

She's sitting right next to the girl, who seems to have survived her ordeal without too much trauma, at least as far as I can tell (and, let's face it, I've never been all that great at reading other people's faces).

She's wearing her previous clothes again, and she has her purse back.

Pseudo-Mom says she's also got my previous clothes, pointing to a paper shopping bag in front of her. She says she's been holding on to our stuff for us, ever since the girl and I ran away from that failed ascension cult ceremony and/or orgy out in the woods.

(Did we really prevent the cult from slipping out of the known world and taking us with them? Or was it just a game, an excuse to have lots of sex and drugs in the countryside? Or could it have worked except, as the Girl once suggested, they'd been doing it wrong?)

I take the bag with me to another room to change.

Besides my own clothes (washed), I've got my wallet back and my now dead cell phone. I could recharge it if I could find a charger here. (Where would the owners have put one? In the kitchen? In the study?)

When I return to the living room, Pseudo-Mom's business partner, the man with the serious anger problem, is also there. He's lying down in the big black recliner chair.

"You do realize," Pseudo-Mom chimed in to me, "that we'd been looking for you two all this time. You're just lucky that we're on the 'dark web' forums for everyone in this neck of the woods who's in the same 'businesses' we're in. We were in the car, with the cell phone Internet—do you KNOW how much extra data COSTS if you go over your plan? And how slow it can get when they decide that they're going to 'throttle' you?

"So, where was I? Oh yeah. We were driving around, doing our other 'business,' waiting for something to come up.

"And sure enough, the couple from this house sent out a notice on several message boards, saying they had a freshly plucked 'bride' to sell. We happened to be not that far away; we were making, eh, 'collections' along this side of the Columbia.

"We got here as quickly as we could. You were already gone. The man of the house was just getting into his car to pick up the woman of the house, who'd been left stranded at a gas station, probably thanks to whatever you did back there. My partner here came up and yelled at him long enough for me to sneak in. You know, there are uses to keep around a man who's naturally angry all the time. He got the big fat guy flustered enough that he just drove off."

The Angry Man just closes his eyes, slouches even further in the recliner chair, and makes a short, non-verbal, gruff growl. He presses a button on one of the chair's arm rests. The whole chair vibrates and makes a dull humming sound.

Pseudo-Mom continues. "And here we are. Cute seeing you again. Have you eaten tonight? I think we can grab something from the kitchen here before we have to split. The people who live here are probably still about five minutes from getting back. Unless they've got a short cut."

I asked Pseudo-Mom if she'd tracked us down because she wanted to try to get the girl working for her again.

The Girl, who'd been silent and poker faced during all of this, quietly tells Pseudo-Mom she doesn't want to return to "the life," especially now, even with a relatively caring boss like Pseudo-Mom instead of abusive creeps like that couple.

"I want to be in a life, in a world, where nobody's trying to buy or sell me, holding me captive, OR (F-word) me over and shoving me out the door. I mean, thanks and all, and I'll never be able to pay you back for saving me and everything. But I really just still want to start my whole life over."

At this point, I expect Pseudo-Mom to reprise her previous sales pitch to the girl from the first night I'd met them. She's going to tell the girl about all the (good) adventures she'd had.

She's going to tell the Girl all about the places she'd been, the friends she'd met, the great (or at least weird/good) sex she'd had with guys she'd never have to have messy "relationships" with, about the money, about all the things she'd bought and can again buy with the money, about the trips and the shows and the festivals and the weed and the clothes and the weed and the shoes and the weed and the wild partying and the weed and the "family" she'd had with Pseudo-Mom and the other girls in Pseudo-Mom's employ.

I expect Pseudo-Mom to remind the girl that if it wasn't for Pseudo-Mom and her partner's dogged work finding her, that the girl would now probably be tied up in the trunk of that SUV (And what does that mean about what was or wasn't in the trunk of the car I'd driven south in? I don't remember hearing any noises from it.)

Then I expect Pseudo-Mom to talk about how the girl would have been sent off to some permanent camp site out in Idaho or wherever, sold off to a "husband" she'd never met before, trying to figure out how to escape that place with nobody like Pseudo-Mom to protect her from who knows what they do to women there, forced to have baby after baby and do housework without appliances, sew all the family's clothes without a sewing machine, cook all the family's meals over an open stove, all under the thumb of some guy who treats her like property.

She doesn't say any of this.

Instead, Pseudo-Mom simply raises her hands in a waving-off motion.

"Hon, if the world of boring stupid 'normal' people seems all that interesting, go ahead. Become a wave slave, working at some burger joint or some big box discount store, never getting enough hours or enough money to live on, having some boring goody two shoes guy for a boyfriend (she doesn't look at me when she says this), hoping that maybe you'll win the lottery and get your picket fence and your two point seven children. If that's all you REALLY want out of life, go ahead and get it. See if I care.

"Besides, it's not you we came all the way out here to retrieve. It's him."

Pseudo-Mom turns to face me again.

"This trim, well-fed, well-bred, sheltered, ignorant, naive young waif here is someone MANY people want to meet. You've already met the Ascension people. They'd really like to try to 'ascend' again, with him as their 'catalyst' again. They claim they've figured out what they've been doing wrong in their previous tries to just vibrate themselves into the next world. They're sure they'll get it done right the next time.

Oh, and there are others who'd also like to partake of this kid's special talents."

I feel, and probably look, about as embarrassed as I've ever felt or looked, at least with my clothes on.

Pseudo-Mom's been looking at me, but talking to the girl about me. Now she talks TO me.

"You're really so blissfully unaware of how unique you are. You probably spent your whole drab existence out in mainstream American consumer-land, not thinking about anything but trying to get your dong into some silly girl's thong. And I'll admit it's an impressive dong, but that's not what everyone wants you for, at least not directly.

"But we can talk about all of that a little later on. I believe the prudent thing for us all to do now is to get the (F-word) out of here before Mr. and Mrs. Goon Squad get back here. Shall we?"

She rises and motions for her partner, the girl, and I to do the same. The Angry Man is the last to get up; the recliner chair's vibrating feature seemed to have relaxed him, at least a little.

We spend just enough time in the kitchen here to find and take anything that looks good for an "eat and run" binge, or rather a "run and eat" binge. Beef jerky, salami sticks, cereal bars, a jug of grapefruit juice. The Angry Man grabs the pimp couple's whiskey bottle.

As we quietly head out the kitchen's exterior door, one or two of the bulldogs fenced up in a back yard awaken. So Mrs. Pimp wasn't lying about those, even if she might have been lying about other features of the house. I can hear the dogs start to yelp and growl. Hell, anyone a quarter mile away can hear these critters.

We all get into what turns out to be the same car I'd first driven south in. Am I ever going to be out of this thing for good, to not ever have to get back in it again?

The Angry Man takes the wheel. It takes him a few tries to get the car to start. He gives out a few common, unimaginative cuss words each time.

These false starts give the Healer Dude, whom I'd completely forgotten about outside, to get out of the still-idling SUV and jump into the car with us. The girl's not happy to see him, to say the least.

But, finally, the car does start.

We get down the curving hillside driveway and off of the property without the pimp couple driving up.

But they see us about a quarter of a mile past the place, make a U turn, and start to chase us.

The Angry Man puts the pedal to the floor. We take off faster than

I thought this white sedan could go. I spill the grapefruit juice I was drinking straight from the bottle.

The Angry Man seems to know some side roads out here that would help us evade the pimp couple in their presumably faster car.

And it's several hours after dark. Everyone else from the church camp weekend will have come home.

Soon, my mother will know something's wrong. If she doesn't know already.

And we're back on the road.

We're back in the first car, the generic white sedan.

Back with the girl, and with Pseudo-Mom and the Angry Man.

And with the Healer Dude, whom the girl still doesn't want to sit next to, and who's even more frozen-scared than before.

We're out who knows where. Does the Angry Man, who's still driving, even know himself where we are?

He says at one point that he knows exactly where we are. But he's not so sure how to get us anywhere else. He says this with a few more standard cuss words mixed into his speech.

The navigation system in this car turns out to be in a "No Signal" zone. (I'm glad I'd never tried to use it.)

Pseudo-Mom tries to use her cell phone to figure out a route. But, as she'd mentioned, her cell company's just "throttled" her, so the maps data is taking forever to load, then just stopping. The phones of the girl, the Healer Dude, and myself are all dead.

I think we're going further and further into the country. We keep running onto what turn out to be dead end roads, or roads that just end at three-way intersections with other roads, or roads that go way down and way up hills with no place to turn off of them, or roads that twist and turn up and down moderate hillsides.

At least a couple of points, the Angry Man slams a fist onto the steering wheel, as if that could accomplish anything.

And at least a couple of points, he's made sudden U-turns (almost into ditches) and taken us back where we'd just been.

In the years before car navigation systems, my mother used to say, you used to hear about guys who got lost driving out in the country and just died of exhaustion and nobody found them until days after.

That probably won't happen to us. Probably.

For one thing, there are people living on these streets. The houses are way far apart from one another, except for the ones in that one subdivision we passed a while back. If we all died from exhaustion, somebody would find us, no later than the next morning.

Oh: and before we died of exhaustion, we could show up at the door of one of these houses, asking them to at least call the police to pick us up. Or, more likely, a tow truck. I don't know if the Angry Man and Pseudo-Mom are that interested in interacting with law enforcement people, ever.

I don't even know if the girl's that trusting of police, given what she used to do.

The Healer Dude is just sitting here in the back seat, crunched up against the right rear car door to the right of me. We may or may not be going even further away from the beloved broken down red pickup of his, just as we're almost certainly going even further away from the home I've been trying to get back to.

The girl is sitting on my lap again, partly (and slightly uncomfortably for me). The one time on this trip that she's deigned to look in the Healer Dude's direction, it was to scowl at the middle-aged man who'd (albeit unwittingly) delivered her to a couple that wanted to enslave and "traffic" her. She won't allow him to feel any less guilty than he obviously does. Ever.

Suddenly, he says something. Very quietly. I'm the only one who even hears it. I tell him to repeat it, louder.

He says we've just passed a landmark he thinks he remembers.

From the driver's seat, the Angry Man snarls that why didn't he speak up before. He makes another sudden U-turn.

The landmark in question is a small, square, wooden building with peeling white paint on the walls. I don't know what it might have originally been built to house, but from the already fading painted signs it was apparently most recently used by something called the Daystar Academy for Spectacular Children. The Angry Dude slows down and stops in front of the place.

The Healer Dude says he remembers the woman who used to own the "academy" had been a patient of his. She'd come to him complaining of stomach pains that just wouldn't go away. He says he'd made all kinds of diagnoses on her and finally gave her a treatment regimen involving ultra-diluted homeopathic tinctures. He says it worked; she stopped feeling the pains within days after starting the tinctures.

I ask if he and her are still in touch.

He says no, and admits a year later she'd found out she'd really had undiagnosed stomach cancer, that had spread to her liver. Stage four.

The girl really glares angrily at him now.

I ask the Healer Dude to forget about all that for a moment, and to tell us how we can get anywhere else from here.

He says the daycare woman had usually come to see him at his "clinic."

But he had been here once. It was in the daytime, of course. But he seems to remember that he'd turned at the first left, or was it the second? And it got him back on the road to the town of Rochester.

The first left turns out to lead just to subdivision cul-de-sacs.

But the second left gets us onto Litterock Road, which gets us onto Sargent Road. Which gets us past a crystal flute store and an animal clinic, and eventually to the main county road that leads us back to the Grand Mound freeway exit.

The Healer Dude sees a tow truck arriving for his busted pickup. He jumps out of the car without saying goodbye.

I move to my right in the back seat. The Girl moves off my left leg, to my relief. Then she gives me a small, brief kiss on my left cheek. She whispers in my ear that she was thanking me for getting that man out of the car where he can't hurt either of us any more.

I ask if Pseudo-Mom and the Angry Man can do anything to help us get to my, and the girl's former, hometown. From the right front seat, Pseudo-Mom raises and waves her right hand. "Let us make like a banana," she says, "and split."

The Angry Man sets us out again. We get back on the freeway. We're going north. So far, so good.

But then he quickly exchanges a glance with Pseudo-Mom.

And then he turns off of the freeway at the very next exit.

He steals a quick glance at Pseudo-Mom's cell phone, which has finally loaded its local maps graphic. He turns us west. He keeps going until we get to a sign announcing the boundary of the "Mima Mounds Natural Area Preserve."

Neither the Angry man nor Pseudo-Mom tell the girl or I anything about what they're doing, or why.

The girl doesn't say anything. She doesn't even make a dirty joke about the name "Mima Mounds." She's just not in a joking mood, or a talking mood, right now. I completely understand how she's feeling.

From what I can see from the car, in the dark, though, the "Mima Mounds" look like a pattern of diagonal rows, consisting of large natural pitcher's-mound like features rising from the earth.

One would not have to be a teenage boy, with the usual levels of raging hormones, to see these as breasts, rising gently and smoothly.

It would probably be a great place to have a one on one outdoor picnic, just the girl and I, perhaps leading to a make out session. Yes, that would be heavenly. In the daytime, of course. In a warmer part of the year. And without the unknown, unstated dangers that continue to loom for both the Girl and me.

We all just sit there in the car, without even any music on. I think about trying to run off again. But I know I can't outrun the car. If Pseudo-Mom really plans to deliver me to someone, perhaps even to the "highest bidder," I can't get out of it right now.

The Girl breaks her silence to whisper a few words to me. She says Pseudo-Mom and her partner never really do anything for anybody else, except for the money.

I am not relieved.

I am even less relieved when the pimp couple drives up beside us in their fancy black convertible, from heading the other way on this road.

The Angry Man at the wheel of this car lowers his front left window and puts his head forward.

The male pimp rolls down his own front left window.

The Angry Man yells loud, insulting things at the pimp husband that I can't fully hear or make sense of from here inside the car. They seem to be resuming whatever angry (naturally) conversation the Angry Man had with the male pimp, back at the pimp couple's house when I was away from it. From where I am, it sounds more like the snapping and snarling of the bulldogs I'd heard back when I left that house the second time.

Then they stop talking. They each re-raise their respective car windows.

The pimps' convertible drives off. All four of us in the white sedan sit silently as we watch its taillights decrease in size and eventually disappear.

Once it's completely gone, Pseudo-Mom speaks up.

"You know, this is an awfully good place to take a hike. No steep slopes. No switchbacks. What do you say we all get out of this cramped space and take a nice late night stroll? You've got your jackets back, and it's briskly cool but not raining."

The Angry Man looks back at us with his usual permanent snort. I guess that means this invitation is more like a command. All four of us get out of the car; the Angry Man is the last to leave, and he locks the car with a beeping fob-key. The beep seems to echo out here in the near nothingness.

Before we start walking, I look out at the nature preserve's flat land with many bumps.

Behind one of the bumps, I think I see a human figure from the waist up, holding a flashlight. Male.

Wait: He looks, from this distance, like someone I've already met. Sort of. Maybe.

22.
HOW DID HE GET HERE?

With Pseudo-Mom and the Angry Man leading the way, the girl and I walk just a short way into the Mima Mounds Natural Area Preserve. The girl and I have been forced to ignore signs prohibiting underground camping and stating that being in here at night constitutes illegal trespassing. The paved trail is a little hard to stay on in the dark, but I quickly learn when my shoes are still on the asphalt and when they're on the damp grass.

The man with the flashlight points it at us. Straight into my eyes, for a second. Then he points it down, showing us the way on the trail toward him.

The Angry Man, who is now more like just a slightly perturbed man, waves to this man. Pseudo-Mom briefly raises a hand toward him.

The man's face is still out of the light.

The man waves at the girl to come further forward, parallel with the two older people. The girl is reluctant.

When I'd first met her, she was so sassy, petulant, likely to spit in the face of anyone who'd try to impose their authority on her.

But now, she's tired of the chase, as I am. It's not fun any more, if it ever was.

I'm weary too. I just want to get into my own bed in my own home and sleep the rest of the week. But I had that chance just hours ago, and I rejected it, because the girl needed me (or so I thought).

And maybe she did, and still does, need me.

Just in case, I hold her hand in mine and walk forward with her. Pseudo-Mom has us stop.

"I apologize that I hadn't told you this before, but I had to make a deal with Mr. and Mrs. Goon Squad." She looks directly at the girl. "I had to tell them I'd at least give you the chance to meet their friend, the Back to Nature Bachelor. I told them I couldn't make you go with him. But I'd let him try to sell himself. Let him make his case as to why he'd like someone to share his lonesome existence. He probably doesn't have a rose to give you, but I'm sure he'll kneel at your feet if you ask him to."

The girl makes one critical look at Pseudo-Mom. Then she makes one eyebrow-raising, eye rolling look at me. I know she's been through some weird stuff. I don't know if this is the weirdest, but it sure could be, or at least come close.

The girl and I walk forward three paces.

The man points his flashlight on the girl, though not directly into her eyes like he'd done with me. In a soft, firm, calm voice, he speaks up to ask her to walk even closer.

We both walk closer.

We're now close enough that I can make out the man's face, even in the darkness.

Him?

HIM?

WHAT THE...

I almost say the F-word silently to myself.

If my reunion with him had happened under literally ANY other circumstances, I'd be happy and relieved to see him.

But as someone who apparently wants, or wanted, to buy himself a "trafficked" sex slave?

I am REALLY not up to compute any of this in my head. And my body's still having flashbacks to the two times it had almost dissolved into thin air.

The girl has to prop me up as I lean over and almost faint.

As she gets me standing again, I look in her eyes. I seem to see a note of concern. Or is it confusion? Like I said before, I'm really bad at sensing these things.

I really don't know what to do next.

I want to run. But that would be futile, probably.

I want to confront him. But how?

I want to—no, I don't know what I want to do.

I want to pass out.

But I don't.

I just stand here.

I wobble a bit, but I stand.

I look again at the girl beside me. She's staring at me, solemnly. She's even more concerned, or more confused, or maybe both.

We're now maybe 30 feet from the man with the very bright flashlight. I can tell he's wearing a decent enough looking, if slightly wrinkled, suit. He points the flashlight directly in my face again.

He looks as surprised to see me as I am to see him.

He only looks a little bit older than I remember. That's odd.

When he last saw me, I was barely through puberty. So if it's taking him a little longer to recognize me than it took for me to recognize him, it's understandable.

He speaks up.

"Is that really YOU?"

I feel like shouting. "YES, it's really ME. Didn't think you'd run into ME, did you? Thought you could just buy yourself a slave sex toy and force her back with you to the sticks of Idaho or wherever and just have your way, raping her and forcing her to have little militia wing-nut babies for you, didn't you? Thought you could get away with it and nobody would notice she was gone or give a (S-word) about her, didn't you? Well, you're not getting away with it! You hear me? I said, DO. YOU. HEAR. ME?"

I feel like rushing toward him like a madman, tackling him, forcing the flashlight weapon from his hand, pinning him to the ground, shoving my fists in his face until he confesses to everything and begs me to stop.

I feel like doing all of those things.

I do none of them.

Instead, I start to stumble again, but stand myself up straight this time. I give him a disapproving scowl, of exactly the kind he used to give me.

"Look: I can explain. It's not what it seems like."

I want to tell him, but don't, that when somebody says, "it's not what it seems like," it's usually exactly what it seems like.

He continues scrambling to try to explain himself.

"I don't know what they told you."

(It doesn't matter which "they" he's talking about.)

"Look: I know that that man and woman like to say things, just to scare people. If they told you I was involved with some right wing militia or whatever, believe me, I'm not. Those people do business online with a lot of people trying to go back to nature. Not just racists. Not just loners sending out mail bombs.

"As for me, I'm simply trying to live simply, off the land, off the grid. Well, as close to 'off the grid' as you can be when everything you need to do with the rest of the world is online.

"And I never intended, I don't intend, to turn anybody into a slave.

"I'm just awfully lonely out there. Oh there are other people in our little community, but it's still a very little group. I need companionship. I need love. Everyone does."

I can't tell if he's lying. But I suspect he could be. Like all the times he lied when he said he'd be at my side, watching my back, forever. Like he said he'd always stay with me, and my sister, and our mother.

He turns the flashlight onto his own face. Harshly lit up from below like that, he looks more desperate than paternalistic.

"Look: I know I haven't been in touch with you lately. But that was all your mother's doing. She doesn't want me to have any part of your or your sister's lives.

"Do you want to know why I REALLY left? It wasn't an affair. And it sure wasn't just because I didn't like her cooking. That would have been the lamest excuse in the world.

"Can't you see? I had to leave. I didn't have any choice in the matter! I couldn't stand what she was trying to turn you into, what she agreed to take part of, the so-called 'destiny' they'd planned for you. Basically from the day you were born. But I couldn't stop them. I couldn't stop her.

"Your whole life: It's been a sham. Don't you see? Haven't you figured it out yet? Think about it. Think about your life. Think about everything that's happened to you. Put the clues together. Add two and two. They won't add up to five."

He might be able to tell his sales pitch and/or apology and/or just plain weird story isn't working on me, not one bit.

He shines the flashlight onto the girl again.

"Please believe me. I'd never hurt a woman, or anyone. I'll never make you do anything you don't want to do. If you want to leave at any time, you can. I don't even have guns. Well, just one. You don't have to say you'll marry me right now. Just say you'll come and look at the place. It's just an hour or so away. We're not outlaws there. We've got all our permits. We've got diesel generators and propane heaters. We're getting an aqueduct built by spring. If you ever want a hot shower, we share a membership in a gym in the next town."

I wonder: How does he know that the Pimp Couple told us he was a militia Neanderthal with no sense of women's independence?

And why are all these people from my life showing up?

Is it because I really was groomed from birth to some sort of "destiny," and all these people are surrounding me, some of them closer than others, to make sure I fulfill whatever the hell that is?

That just sounds TOO weird. Even by the standards of weirdness I've been living in these past three days (going on four).

He walks toward us. He tries to shake my hand, and then embrace me. I just stiffen up in his arms. I don't return his gesture of reunion.

I turn my head a sharp right to look at the girl beside me. She leans in my direction with her eyebrows up and her mouth partly open. She reaches out her left hand to touch my back.

So she IS concerned.

But I'm just confused.

And now the man is walking away from us. But he's waving his flashlight, silently inviting us to follow him.

From in back of us, the Angry Man and Pseudo-Mom walk forward. I turn around to see them shooing us to also walk forward, following the man.

Damn, I really, really don't want to do this. And neither does the girl.

But we seem to be doing it anyway.

Why?

23.
WHAT'S THIS SUPPOSED TO BE?
WHO'S HE SUPPOSED TO BE?

It's Tuesday morning, just before the overcast sunrise. I'm missing from home. In less than an hour I'll be missing from school.

And I'm even further away from home than I was at the last sunset.

I open a thin curtain over a small window to look out.

From the outside, when we drove up, this place was just a driveway surrounded by trees on the end of an old narrow road, with a fading PRIVATE PROPERTY sign and a wooden gate he had to get out of the car to open, get back in and drive past, then get out again to close. He says it used to be a year-round logging camp.

From the inside, late last night, it was a clearing with some small structures and some dirt roads and trails leading further into the woods. When he stopped the car and the headlights went out, I could see almost nothing.

From this window, now, I still can't see all that much.

Just the outlines of some shacks and trailers, and a couple of parked vehicles in addition to the car we came here in.

The trip out here in his beater Malibu took about an hour, maybe a little less. None of us talked during any of it.

Because the girl didn't want to sleep in the same "tiny house" as him, he let us use the RV (on blocks) of someone who's not here right now. It was unlocked. If there were any working lights, if there was any running water, if there was any heat, we couldn't find them. We did find a single bed, with no sheets or covers. We took turns sleeping on it and on the floor, dressed.

The RV reeks inside of something I don't know. If the girl knows, she's not telling me, not yet anyway.

She might have gotten some sleep, off and on, during the past few hours. I sure didn't get much.

At one point she came down and joined me lying on the floor. When I awakened and felt her curling up next to me, I took it as my cue to stand and get onto the small bed.

I wonder what my mother and sister are doing. Will anyone at school notices I'm gone?

If I'm lucky, the police will start to look for me. Even though

I'd heard that someone has to be missing for three days before the police will start looking. That may be a media myth, though. Especially for a juvenile case.

I wonder if I'll be the subject of one of those "Amber alerts." (And why aren't they red? "Amber" is a weird color for an alert, isn't it? And why am I suddenly thinking about this?)

The sky is starting to turn from dark blue to gray.

The local landscape is coming into detail.

This place looks perfect, in all its imperfections.

That may be what makes it so creepy.

Some of the shacks look like "tiny houses." Some look like the pre-fab shacks you get at the big-box hardware stores. Some look, well, just like shacks.

There are a couple of prefab buildings on one end of this dirt clearing. One of them is made of wood and looks like a "portable" classroom building; the other is made of corrugated steel.

There are, of course, no streetlights or floodlights.

The man's car, in the light, looks even more decrepit than it sounded during the night. His "tiny house" looks like an oversized dollhouse or a shrunken cottage.

I can hear the girl who's been traveling with me getting up, yawning, and yelling about where the (F-word) is there any coffee. (One more drug she's not given up. I won't, I can't, judge her on it.)

She shrieks briefly and calls out my name. I turn around.

In the dim light, I see the walls of this small RV are papered floor to ceiling with pictures cut out from old porn mags.

And, as far as I can tell from a quick glance, every single image has the model's eyes and genitals cut out.

I see a pair of scissors and an X-Acto knife (with a box of blades) on the small kitchen table, along with some rubber cement.

I look at the girl again. She stares silently, tracking her eyes across all the doctored pictures.

Then she laughs. A huge howl.

It's been a while since I've seen her be the sassy, cynical girl she was when I first saw her.

But we've still got to get out of here.

There's no coffee and very little food here in the RV. There are a few tea bags and a kettle and a range top. It runs on gas. The gas isn't on.

We stumble outside of the place.

The man who drove us here shows up outside the RV with steaming cups of coffee, and invites us back to his tiny house. He's wearing different, far rougher and older, clothes today.

The man says the guy with the RV is a good man, but a little off, like some of the people here, especially the ones who stay here year round. He says he often goes off for a week or two, especially during mushroom season. He always comes back when he needs a hot meal and a change of clothes. The man says the RV guy had only been gone this time for a night or two, so he knew he wouldn't be right back.

Before we can descend the cinder block steps of this RV, an old man shuffles out from the woods, toward and in a shack. He's got a bald spot, a long white beard, and a prominent beer belly. He's wearing worn sneakers, dirty white socks, and no other clothing. Yes, on a cold morning in January. The girl beside me doesn't scream. She's probably seen worse.

Another harmless eccentric? I ask.

He says yes. He says the Naked Guy, for that's what they all call him here, is supposed to at least wear shorts whenever visitors are expected on the premises. He says the Naked Guy always heads out to the stream for a brisk morning dip at sunrise; but he often walks around naked, like just whenever.

My hesitations about this place just grow. I'm sure the girl's hesitations about it grow likewise.

Before we've walked ten paces toward the man's tiny house, a small three legged dog runs toward us, yipping away. Nothing we can do can shut it up or make it let us pass. The man makes a non-verbal guttural noise and the dog sits. We walk around it.

Before anything else can cross our path, we make it to the narrow door of the tiny house. There's a gas or propane powered generator at its side and an antenna type thing surrounded by a Pringles can attached to the sloping roof. The man says that's his Wi-Fi antenna, pointed in the direction of the communal transmitter at the "community house," which in turn is fed by a satellite hookup.

He warns us that cell phones don't work here (which is moot since both mine and the girl's are out of power) as we enter the house.

The man's tiny house is no TARDIS, that's for sure. It's just as cramped within as it looks like it is from without.

It's decorated in Late Bachelor Studio Apartment style. There's a sagging futon couch and a small table with a laptop computer, next to an old folding metal chair. He does seem to have cleaned the living room/kitchen recently.

The man serves us eggy breakfast Hot Pockets, from the small microwave in his mini kitchen.

He tells me the people here today are just the year-round residents. He says other people "winter" in cities or nearby towns, or in motels on the coast that have lower winter rates. Anyplace with, you know, central heating and hot water. Then they come back here to live four to eight months a year.

He says some of them make their living making handcrafted arts products. He shows me some of them, on the little table and hung on the walls and in pictures on his laptop. They include:

• An abstract portrait of Jesus made from different-colored bottle caps.

• A belt with several sets of chicken-foot bones dangling from it.

• A rusty mattress spring "repurposed" as wall art.

• Earrings with old computer floppy discs hung from them. necklace made of what look like metal scraps.

• And a line of T-shirts, in adult and child sizes, "hand painted" (as the man insists) with what the man calls "stylized" (I'd just call them awkward) caricatures of dead Hollywood movie stars depicted as happy ghosts.

Then he punches up another image on the laptop. It's a (competently drawn) rendering of what the man says this place is intended to eventually look like.

He zooms in on various parts of the image.

Instead of the big dirt and gravel clearing in the middle of the camp, there's a beautifully landscaped garden. It's surrounded by small, but professionally designed, cabins and cottages. There's a Native "longhouse" style "community building," next to a small building with a GENERAL STORE sign. There are solar panels and modern power-generating windmills and rain water collection tubs. The man says there would also be a solar powered water heater, and pumps and pipes bringing water down from the creek just outside the clearing.

He then brings up a second drawing, depicting how the lands just beyond this clearing would look.

There's one cleared trail leading to a "fire circle," with a rock-enclosed campfire pit surrounded by split-log benches.

Another trail leads to the aforementioned creek, with a covered hot tub (presumably fed by the creek) and a wooden deck with an outdoor co-ed shower. The man says, though it's not in the drawing, that the group could even build its own "fish friendly hydro generator" on the creek.

A third trail leads to another clearing in the woods, where a larger garden is planted with assorted vegetable plants.

I notice a date on this drawing—2010.

The man explains the two drawings to us, with a light in his eyes and a pep in his voice I hadn't noticed yet in this visit.

This, he says, is what this was originally intended to be. Before some of the original team burned out and split, and the others "just drifted into their own hermit lives."

The old idea, he says, was to make this an "intentional community," where people would live off the grid, off of the land. A communal farm would produce quality organic veggies, supporting the community's expenses. There would also be writers' and artists' retreats, weekend educational camps for kids, "burner" camps, and even "alternative religious" ceremonies.

Since I'd just barely gotten out of an "alternative religious" ceremony with my life, I silently shudder to myself. If the man said earlier that he knows my intended "destiny," then he probably ought to know I'm not too keen on "alternative religious" ceremonies right now.

The man notices my apprehension. He finally notices something I feel.

"Don't you worry. You'll be safe here. I won't let those groups that have their plans for you get anywhere near you." Did he say "groups," plural?

"Can't you see, this is the perfect place for you. The perfect hideout. They can't find you here. And even if they tracked you down, nobody can get in except by the locked gate."

Wait a minute, I think: If the gate's locked, and nobody can get in who's not supposed to, how do the girl and I get out? Are we stuck on the man deciding to let us out? He doesn't sound like he wants to let me go. Maybe not the girl either.

The man starts to get a little manic.

"And you'd be our secret weapon here, as it were. You could help me get these introvert individualists to work together again, to make this place what it was supposed to be."

Then he turns to the girl beside me.

"If you want to be with him and not with me, I understand. If you ever change your mind, you know I'll always welcome you.

"And I know I said you can leave anytime." He says this to the girl directly, not to me.

"But now that I've slept on it, I think you really ought to give it a try here. At least through the summer. It's a lot more active here in the summer. If, after that, you still want to go…"

The man's glaring at her. He seems to have plans for her that go beyond simply having sex. He really does want to own her. And he wants to own me, for different purposes.

The girl looks at me. We both know we've got to get back out of here. Somehow. Even if it means disappearing the same way the guy with the freaky pictures in his RV disappears.

Or, perhaps, the same way I've already almost disappeared.

24.
AM I NO BETTER THAN THEM?

It's a little later the same morning. The man who'd brought us here, who had a relationship with me in the past and now wants one in the future, has sent an email to everyone currently living in the camp, to have us meet them. (I don't feel like calling this camp a "community," because it doesn't seem like a group of people working and living together.)

He lets me and the girl who's traveling with me to rest a bit on the saggy futon in his Tiny House. He leaves for just a little while. I try to get on his laptop computer, to try to get a message out to my mother and sister back home. The machine's password protected. People leave their doors unlocked out here, but they lock up their computers?

I sit back on the futon just as the man comes back in. He says they're ready to meet us.

The camp's Community Center is a decrepit old portable classroom building. It's unheated. About a dozen men and one woman sit on office surplus chairs of various shapes and sizes, set up in a small circle. There are art and craft works in progress on old folding office tables by the walls of the room, looking about as unsalable as the works I'd already seen. There's a bulletin board just inside the door, on which are tacked up printouts of various messages to the residents, asking them to not leave their trash strewn around or defecate in the creek.

All the year-round residents of the camp have gathered to meet us. Or most of them. The man says there are two or three guys who never leave their shacks or trailers, at least not before late afternoon.

Before we get seated, the man whispers to us in the doorway about some of the people who ARE in the room.

First, he tells us about the gun nut, who points his rifle straight at us. The man tells us the gun nut points it at everyone, known or unknown to him. The man says the gun nut's daughter came by once a year or so ago and disabled his rifle by taking a firing bolt out of it, but the gun nut doesn't seem to know and/or care.

Seated right next to the gun nut, there's a 40-ish man swigging bargain brand whiskey straight from the plastic jug in one hand, and chain-smoking cigarettes from the other hand. A couple of empty chairs away from him there's a 30-ish guy who seems to be in a world of his own, with dilated eyes and a blank smile. The man next to us tells us that that guy's a "popper" head. The man adds that the camp had originally been intended to be clean and sober, but after a while...

On the other side of the circle of chairs are couple of 35-ish guys who look like they might be on the run from the law, or are simply total loners. The man tells me they make a lot of the art and craft works he'd shown to us.

Scattered elsewhere in the circle of chairs are a guy in a JESUS CHRIST embroidered baseball cap; a stringy-haired guy who's nodding off; the Naked Guy (who, possibly reluctantly, has put on cut-off jeans for this meeting); a guy with a worn sweatshirt with a logo that looks like it could either signify neo-Nazis or Queer Nation or the Klingon empire; and one and only one woman—a woman with a gaunt face and thin hair, missing at least one front tooth, stooped over, with an expression of someone who'd been through Hell and still isn't completely beyond it.

The man walks us to the center of the room, with the chairs surrounding us. He introduces us as the newest full time residents of the "community."

Everyone stares, and glares, at us.

I feel as "naked" as I'd felt at the ascension orgy cult, when the Girl and I really were naked.

The man tells the other hermits about everything he says we've agreed to do, to prove our worthiness to be part of the "community." We've agreed to none of them.

As the man continues hyping our supposed new status as the young girl and boy who will bring this "community" back to its originally intended goals (which sounds like what he'd said other people had planned for me as my life's "destiny"), I try to mouth the words "HELP US PLEASE" while the man's not looking my way.

I look at the girl beside me. She's not AS uncomfortable as I am, but that's not saying much. She's probably more used than I am to being ogled at by guys who have plans for her.

Oh. My. God.

Is that what the man expects her to be?

That would mean she's in as much trouble here as I am.

With the man's short speech quickly done (he seems to know these people's attention spans), the hermits stand up and swarm around us, sizing us up. Many of them size the girl up, closely, from head to toe. A few of them size me up, closely, from head to toe.

One or two of them seem to see me as one of them.

Oh dear.

One of them specifically looks over my body the same way that others of them are looking over the girl's body.

Oh dear, oh dear, oh (F-word) dear.

While I'm obsessed about myself like that, the Girl pulls me aside.

She tells me the one woman in the room had come up to her while I wasn't looking. She says the older woman could represent what the girl herself could become if the Girl doesn't, as she obsessively wants to, turn her life around.

She tells me the old woman said she wanted the girl to join her, or take her place, as the "town mistress."

Or did the Girl really say "the town mattress"?

I guess it's the same either way.

And anyway, we've got to get out of here.

Wherever "here" really is.

And however we can do it.

How the (F-word) will we do it?

I'm still trying to sort it out as we leave the little portable building.

The man calls on us to follow him back to his Tiny House, but we don't.

We just stand here, in the middle of the dirt and gravel clearing.

We don't look at or talk to any of the hermits, some of who are beginning to circle around us.

I feel a single rain drop from the overcast sky. Then another. I don't scramble for shelter and neither does the Girl.

Did all the traveling we've done lately lead just to this dead end? It's not right! There's got to be more than just this.

The girl grabs my upper sides, to force me to look at her.

She says she knows I'm itching to get out of here.

But she says we should be, as she puts it, "sneaky" about it.

The people here, she tries to say delicately, are, well, delicate. She says we don't want to needlessly "rustle" their tender emotions.

I agree. Some of these guys I don't want to make mad, or even make too excited.

I tell her she's right. She gives me an "aren't I always" glance and a slightly haughty pose. (Am I finally becoming good at reading faces and body language? At least HER face and body language?)

She also says these people need to stay here. They wouldn't make it in the outside world. But here, they can be their own extended family; protecting each other as well as they know how.

Then I tell her that I've had a feeling all morning.

Having seen what's become of the man who brought us here, a man who shares a big part of my past upbringing, and then seeing these other guys—it all makes me feel that, if I stay here, I'll become just like them. Whatever form of crazy this is, it'll get into me, building slowly, until it's taken me over. I tell the Girl it'll happen to her too.

The Girl says she already knows. She talks about the one woman here, the one who wants the Girl to take over as the camp's sex worker.

"She looks exactly like I'll look if I fail to turn my life around. Spent. Used up. Drained of all life."

So we've got to get out.

But how?

If we try to run down the narrow little road we were driven up here on, the man who'd driven us here can easily drive back down and catch up with us. He could have some of these "emotionally challenged" people join in to overtake us.

If we wait until dark, we could just end up getting lost in the local woods.

No, I say, our best chance is to try to follow whatever trails the mushroom guy had used to "just disappear" from the camp.

Even if it runs the risk of, you know, meeting the mushroom guy, with his weird (to say the least) attitude toward women.

25.
IS THIS THE ANSWER,
OR JUST ANOTHER SET OF QUESTIONS?

It's no wintertime drizzle.

It's a serious downpour.

And it's been going on at least a half hour.

And it's just warm enough to not snow.

It's no weather to be outside in.

But that's where we are.

Sort of.

Where we are, we can hear the rain pouring down. But we can't see it. We can see that it's still light (or rather gray) out.

We'd been walking up one trail, then another, then another, roughly trying to get where a road might be. (My guess: uphill paths would likely go further into the forest; downhill paths would get us back at least to farm country.)

The girl who's with me has had about as much strength and stamina for this hike as I've had. Maybe a little more.

We'd done this for about an hour and a half since we'd snuck out of the "intentional community." Then when the rain started to get seriously serious, we stopped at this thing.

As far as we know, nobody's come after us.

The rain is noisy. But it's a calming noise, a hypnotic noise.

The aging wood roof of this shack looks worn, but somehow it's still watertight.

The Girl says it could have been a storage shed for a logging camp. There used to be a lot of little timber "company towns" and year-round camps around places like this.

The shed's front door still opens and closes easily. There's just a little rust on the hinges.

The thing is big enough for both of us to lie down on the wood floor; though we're both sitting down now. She's in a perfect lotus position. I'm sitting a little more awkwardly.

She says she can smell the lingering scent of weed in here. My sense of smell isn't that great; and she knows that scent better than I do. This could very well be where the mushroom guy from the "community" crashes when he's out on his own.

Certainly somebody's been using the shed lately. There's a relatively newly installed closing latch here on the inside. There's a blanket, inefficiently folded up in a corner of the floor. Outside, there's a small latrine and a beaten-up plastic trash bin. Inside the latter are relics that indicate various junk food items were consumed here recently.

The Girl and I go through a long moment of silence together.

Then she sighs and says if she weren't so obsessed with sobriety, she'd try to find some magic mushrooms herself. I know I wouldn't try. I have no clue at all how to tell the regular, the druggy, and the poison ones apart.

I ask her what a mushroom high feels like. She says there are no paranoid effects. There's no harshness. Everything seems calm, happy, and giddy. You see the subtle patterns of whatever's around you as really prominent, really obvious.

She says this would be a perfect place to do them. You feel like the countryside is a part of you and you a part of it. She says you feel like you're one with all the plants and the animals. Other people, you don't feel so close to—at least if they're not tripping with you.

No, I tell her. I've never had any experience like that.

That recent time with the energy healer dude was the closest I'd had to that. And even with that, as I remind her (even though she was there and saw it all), I didn't feel connected to the world around me. Just the opposite. I felt like I'd almost dissolved out of my body, out of the physical world.

I tell her I wish I could do that here, only with her with me, and with the ability to reappear at someplace safe, preferably at my home. Preferably with clothes to wear when we reappear.

The Girl suggests we try to induce such a state with hypnosis, which she's been learning to help her stay sober. Hey, it can't hurt, right? Anything to relieve the state of constant apprehension I've been in today.

With the Girl instructing me in self-hypnosis, and with the raindrops on the shack's roof as a soundtrack, I sit up straight with my back against the shack's wall. I close my eyes. I breathe in and out, slowly. I rest my hands in my lap.

As she instructs, I concentrate on, then relax, one area of my body after another. I imagine myself going deep into a relaxed state, then deeper, then deeper still.

She asks me to imagine I'm in a warm, safe, relaxing, comforting place. She suggests I think about a warm beach on a summer's day. I try. It doesn't work.

I think of my bedroom back home in the wee hours of the morning. My own bed; my own covers. That works. I can almost smell the Glade Plug-In and the fabric softener and my regular shampoo.

Now, she asks me to feel all the sensations I'd felt when I'd begun to vibrate out of my body. How it felt in every limb, every organ, every lobe of my brain, in my mind, in my heart, in my soul.

I mentally re-enact the whole thing. From the silent "buzzing" across my skin, to the incredible lightness, to the total relaxation, to the sense that I was leaving the world, to the reaction of total panic, to my forcing myself, with the Girl's help, to shut the process down.

Re-living that part essentially wakes me from my trance. I open my eyes.

She looks at me with a calm, centered, caring face. Softly, she suggests we try again. Only this time, we'll simply try to relax and think of good things; supportive things; things that make me feel good. She says she'll do the same.

With her voice leading, with the rain sound lightening up a little, we start over.

This time it's easier for me to "go deep."

Again, she brings me to my "safe place." My place of warmth, of comfort, of centeredness, of wisdom.

Only this time it's a bit more abstract. It's a bed, in a room, but it's not my bedroom. It's some other room in some other building.

And I'm not alone in there.

She's here.

Like she's been here for me, and me for her.

I see her in my mind and I feel stronger. I feel more confident. I feel like a different person. No—more like a "me" that had been hidden before.

What I don't feel: Not the animal lust that I was induced/drugged into back at the ascension orgy service. Not the pure bodily discover I'd felt back with the co-pastor Friday night. Something else. Something strange. Something even stranger than anything I've been through these past few days.

What do I call what I feel with her?

Does it matter whether I have a name for it or not?

It doesn't.

That's the one answer I clearly know.

The trance-image of her I see in my mind merges with the "real" her who's talking to me quietly and serenely from a few feet away.

They both gently lead me up, out of my trance, back to the allegedly "real" world. A world in which I feel more alive, more composed, than I may ever have before.

When I finally open my eyes, she is right next to me, gazing into my eyes. I don't turn away. But she does. She says she has to go get something.

She efficiently stands up and retrieves her purse. She fishes around in it and retrieves a plastic square with a raised circle inside it.

"Squaring the circle." Isn't that some impossible math problem?

Yes, I remember in geometry class. You can only get a close answer, not a perfect solution. It involves pi, that great "transcendental irrational number."

She does a very irrational thing but a perfect solution. She takes me by both hands and leads me onto the floor of the shed. She climbs on top of me. She removes her jacket, then her shirt. She kisses me—not aggressively like the first time with her, but tenderly, deeply, and passionately. I hold her breasts in my hands. They feel familiar, like a place I was always intended to be. My new "home," as it were.

She gets back up. Silently, she takes off her other garments and spreads the blanket (thankfully not an itchy one) on the shed floor. I also undress. We lie down on the blanket together.

We explore our and one another's bodies. Every inch of skin kissed, rubbed, licked.

She introduces me to her "sacred place" (not a phrase I'd learned in church, one I've just made up). It feels and tastes exquisite. As I do this, she takes my lower part into her mouth again. This time slowly and carefully. During this, she applies the condom.

She climbs atop me and lowers her lower area onto mine.

The only previous time I'd done this, I'd been manipulated, used. I didn't recognize it at the time because it was all so new and exciting. But now I know. It's so much better when you're with someone who sincerely cares about you, and you for her. But if it weren't for that first time, I'd never have THIS time, this person, this young woman who's opening her heart to me as well as her body.

She clearly knows what she's doing. By adjusting the pace and intensity of her moves, she's able to keep me "unspent" for what seems like an eternity.

When my anxious, hormonal teenage body finally gives in, she lifts herself up. She removes the condom and licks up all of my, er, discharge. Then she lies down beside me.

I tell her I hope I'd been good, considering my lack of (much) experience.

She says she'd been inexperienced too. Inexperienced at "really making love." Oh, she'd (F-word)ed a lot. But that was all mercenary, for the money. If any of that sex was any good for her, and it sometimes was, that was a bonus. But she'd never done it with anyone she cared about, until now.

She says she knew we would be lovers when I came back to the survivalist pimp couple's house. I could have just left her there, but I didn't. She says it's the first huge, unselfish thing anyone had done for her in a long time. She says her Pseudo-Mom, and that woman's business partner the Angry Man, never did anything, for her or anybody, that wasn't really for the money.

The talking subsides. We lie intertwined as the raindrops on the shed's roof taper off.

We don't have to tell each other that we should resume trying to get back to civilization.

We're barely re-dressed when we hear the shed's door rattling. Someone's trying to get in.

We stand in back of the door as I undo the inside latch.

Will it be the mushroom eating guy with the disturbing apparent attitude about women?

Will it be the man who'd brought us to the "intentional community," out to return us there and keep us there?

I take a peek through the just-barely-open door.

It's neither of those.

26.
WHAT'S HE TURNED INTO NOW?

It's a little after 3 p.m. on this car's clock. The Girl and I are on the road again, again. In the back seat again, again.

This became tiresome, and then some, a while ago. I really, really want it to end.

At least this car's a different one. It's a red domestic sports car, late model, with the soft-top up. The girl traveling with me (who is now something more and different than just that, but I don't have words for it) calls it "a male-midlife-crisis-mobile." It's good to hear her being cynical again. It means, I now know, that she's getting her spirit back in gear.

Turned out the shed we'd hidden from the rain in was just a half-mile or so from a road. That's the shed where these people found us. They'd been acting on instructions phoned in by the girl's Pseudo-Mom and her business partner, who'd suspected something would be unsafe for us at the "intentional community."

(The subdivision I live in was originally advertised as a "planned community," but that's a completely different thing. And why am I thinking of THAT now?)

Just where Pseudo-Mom and her partner the Angry Man are now, I haven't a clue.

Where I am, I have a little more knowledge; but just a little. We're not going to my home. We're wandering through the countryside again. We've just turned off of Highway 12, onto another county road.

Under other circumstances, I might have felt spiritually refreshed by these landscapes of forests, two-lane roads, farms, tiny towns, out-of-season produce stands, even the occasional deer. But not this time.

Just now, a stray cow meanders onto the road, a ways ahead of us. The man driving the car suddenly hits the brakes. We skid on the damp pavement and come to a stop at least 30 feet away from the cow. The driver curses at the cow as if the cow could hear him. When the cow is safely across the road, the driver hits the gas pedal hard. We almost hydroplane above the road; he's going so fast.

Our driver this time is the first man I'd met on this long misadventure. The short man with a small angular nose and skinny fingers. He's wearing another loose-fitting casual suit (brown this time) and a button-down white shirt with a tie that doesn't really match the suit.

The woman who was with him when I first met him is with him now, in the front passenger's seat. She's somewhat less "formally" dressed as he is. Green slacks, canvas shoes, and a blue sweatshirt over a green shirt. She looks at him periodically, disapprovingly, particularly when he drives too aggressively for her tastes.

Earlier, when they'd found us in the shed, it was the man who wolf-whistled and said he could hear us making love "and it sounded really hot, man." The woman shoved a sharp elbow in his side.

The woman looks back and sees the girl, who normally has always looked so tough, leaning on my shoulder. She says we look so cute. The girl, who would normally lash out harshly at anyone who accused her of being "cute," simply, silently turns her head away from the woman.

The woman says it's good that I've met the Girl. "Every man, when he's just becoming a man, needs someone to show him and the major and minor parts about being a man. That's what I'm doing with him." He's only learning to "be a man" at HIS age?

Then the woman thanks me for "bringing down his hormone meds. Don't ask me why you can get them more easily in Washington than in Oregon. Just one of those mysteries, I guess."

So THAT's what was in the trunk of the car that first day. At least I've helped somebody during all this mess.

But that would mean my female co-pastor, who'd started me on all this, knows this man somehow.

But does that mean she knows—

Don't try to think about it. Just don't.

Now the woman's back to talking about her relationship with the man next to her.

"The man he used to be with (probably the one I've been calling the Angry Man), that relationship ended when he (the man now driving this car) realized he didn't want to be WITH HIM, he wanted to BE HIM. An alpha male, a boss, a man who said what he meant and got what he wanted.

"I admire him so much. He gave up everything he was, to become everything he is. But he can still be a real pain sometimes. He still hasn't learned a lot of the subtleties."

During this, the skinny-fingered man himself stays silent except for an occasional growl, not that different from the grumblings I've heard from the Angry Man. He seems not to like to have his secrets talked about like this.

That woman's still keeping some secrets from me, though.

I ask her why we didn't get in the freeway a while ago; why we're not going where the Girl and I need to go.

"But you ARE going where you need to go."

The woman says she and the skinny-fingered man have specific instructions from Pseudo-Mom to deliver the girl and me to someone who will "make you do what you need to do."

That "destiny" thing again?

Or, perhaps more likely, Pseudo-Mom found a new "highest bidder" for me and this "gift" I never wanted to have, that I still don't understand.

I realize it's no use to grill her any further on this subject. All, as the cliché goes, will be revealed in due time.

Due time turns out to be just ten minutes later.

We pull into a long, paved, unmarked driveway. I now lean on the shoulder of the girl next to me as the car slows to a stop.

It's flat here. This plot of land might have been a farm before it became whatever it is now.

And what is it now?

I just see a field of grass here. And some other cars and trucks and a motorcycle parked here in front. Another alternative revival meeting?

No, I soon realize. It's a regular old style revival meeting.

Or is it?

I see some Fundamentalist Christian slogans on bumper and window stickers here.

But I also see other stickers, with words and images I don't know.

Gradually, the girl and I see various, casually and seasonally dressed, men and women approach this car we're still in.

They seem to be forming a "periphery," like plainclothes bodyguards, around one old man in the middle.

As this circle walks closer to us, I try to see who the old man in the center is.

Oh no.

Oh (F-word) no.

It can't be.

But it is.

And I should have known it all along.

The highest bidder indeed.

27.
DOES HE REALLY THINK THIS WILL WORK?
AND WHAT IF IT DOES?

These people are far more prudish than the ascension orgy people. The girl I'm traveling with and I get to keep our own clothes on, beneath the black robes they've supplied for us.

We're in the middle of a grassy field. There's no stage, no tent. Not even a little platform of shipping pallets.

They tell me it's a full moon tonight, even a Super Moon, whatever that is; perfect conditions for what they want to do. Not that you could tell, with the cloud cover only starting to break up now, just before sunset.

It turns out it was the Girl who first recognized the old man who's running this ceremony or whatever it is. She'd first shuddered and cringed at the sight of him. Then she lowered and shook her face, in either pity or "schadenfreude" (I think that's the term) over his current decrepit state.

He walks only sluggishly, sometimes relying on two athletic-looking men to hold him up.

He can barely keep his eyes open.

His scowling face, which I once thought was the ultimate expression of righteous power, now looks more like one of those old doll heads made from withered dried fruit.

The arms he used to forcefully outstretch from the pulpit, to scare his parish about the "long reach of the devil's hand," he now can barely lift.

His two beefy companions motion for the Girl and I to walk toward them, rather than make him walk any further.

In a voice that's more gravelly than I remember, he says I've grown into a fine looking young man. He says he can sense that I'm "pure and righteous." I don't say anything to contradict him.

He barely notices the girl. When he finally looks her way, he squints his bifocal-equipped eyes. Then he grumbles something about "a Jezebel, daughter of a Delilah, wicked harlot, scarlet sinner."

Then he makes a sickening, dirty-old-man grin. "Perfect. This is precisely what we need. The transference is assured."

I yell at him. I tell him I've just found out what he did to all the girls in the church, possibly including my own sister. And even to some of the boys. I ask him how he can live with himself after all he's done?

The old man doesn't understand what I'm talking about, or pretends he doesn't.

Again, I tell him he's no man of God. He's nothing more than a serial child rapist. A pathetic old criminal.

He seems to have conveniently forgotten about what he'd done. He stares at me, lost in confusion.

But then he sternly says that he'd been "unfairly persecuted by agents of Satan on Earth" (i.e., the board of deacons who'd fired him from his own church), in retaliation for his having "driven the Devil out of so many innocent women and youths."

I yell, loudly enough that everyone on this grassy lot can hear, "Don't you know you did something wrong?"

He raises his stooped head and shoulders toward me. "Yes. I did something wrong. I did several things wrong. I was wrong about so many things."

He says he was wrong to spend so many years with his mind, and his pastoral message, stuck in an unwavering, unquestioning obedience to standard-issue Fundamentalist theology.

But since then, he says, he's studied the works of the Christian mystics, the Coptics, the mystery schools of Jesus' time, Theosophy, Kabbalah, the threefold and fivefold paths, the doctrine of transforming the self. It all led, he pronounces, to his developing his own doctrine. He says he calls it "apocalyptic esotericism."

So, like the man who drove me here, this man has re-invented himself.

I say nothing but let him rant on, in an alternately hesitant and pugnacious (is that a real word?) tone.

He says that during the long lonely days of his enforced retirement, he'd begun to question the traditional Fundamentalist doctrines of the Rapture and the End Times.

And he came to the conclusion: He had been wrong.

Wrong to believe the Antichrist, the earthly incarnation of Satan, would appear as the ultimate Communist liberal.

And wrong to try to prevent the Antichrist's incarnation among us.

No, he claims, "Satan's realization in the physical world must be in the guise of the ultimate Christian conservative! A man who will easily lead many of Christ's truest believers astray, tempting them into abandoning the path of the sacred in favor of the easy, treacherous pursuits of wealth and worldly power. A man who will fan the flames of wars and ethnic hatreds around the world. A man who will hasten the destruction of the lands and the waters, all in the name of greed. A man who will use physical, psychological, and spiritual tools to bring the establishment of Hell on Earth."

His voice now sounds like the forceful "fire and brimstone" speaker I remember. But his words this time are different, confusing.

"That, my young friend, is not a destiny to be prevented, but one to be made more imminent! We must hasten the arrival of Hell on Earth, so we can hasten the subsequent arrival of Heaven on Earth."

And, as I'd feared but expected, he says I will play a role in this process.

"You are a special young man. Pure of mind and heart." (He doesn't mention whether I'm "pure" of body, which I'm not any more, at least by the old definition he used to use.)

"You have a righteous soul—but a soul that is only tenuously attached to your physical body.

"You will be the perfect receptacle for the Evil One.

"The world will continue to see you as, and believe that you are, the same clean minded, righteous follower of our Lord that you have been until tonight.

"But, deep within you, so deep that even you might not immediately perceive it, the spirit of the Prince of Darkness himself will lie fallow, awaiting that fearful day when he will arise to claim, first your body and then the souls of all the heathen."

Ah, great. Somebody else who's got plans for me that I don't want to live up to.

I look at the girl, who's been by my side and has heard the old man's pronouncements.

For the first time, she seems not cynical, not weary, not bored.

Just frightened.

28.
CAN WE STOP THIS?
CAN WE START THAT?

The "rite of transference" has begun, as the sky grows dark. The clouds have mostly parted. The stars will be out tonight, here far away from competition with the city's light.

The Girl and I have been told where to stand, but not what we are to do—or what others will do to us.

The man and woman who'd driven us here, and the red convertible they'd driven us here in, seem to be gone.

I now recognize some of the people here in this grassy field. They're some of the Calvary Fellowship church members, who'd quit when the old man was forced out. They've either stuck with him or found their way back to him.

I vaguely remember some of them as the more aggressively obedient members of the flock. The old women, middle aged couples, and young jock-type men who'd shouted "Amen!" the loudest during his old sermons, who'd stared the most disapprovingly at members who'd skipped going even one Sunday, who'd complained the most when someone in Sunday School made even an innocent question about the church's doctrines.

Now they're standing out here (except the ones who can't stand up for long periods of time; they have chairs). They're in black robes, standing in a circle. On the front of each robe is a different mystic symbol of some sort. I have no idea what any of them are or what they mean.

There are maybe 23 people total around the circle.

Some of them hold up torches, as they slowly chant something that sounds like it could be sampled on a "chillout" electronic dance track.

Others beat loud drums, in unison, in a slow rhythm.

Within the circle, arranged on the points of a short, triangle-shaped wood platform, are the old man and his two assistants/bodyguards. A microphone stand and a battery-powered speaker are in front of the old man.

Another triangle could be drawn between him, the girl, and me, standing separately in front of him on two other triangular platforms.

A triangle inside a circle. What's that the logo of?

Is it the symbol of the AA meetings that use the church's basement some weeknights? Maybe.

Is it one of the "freemason" symbols the old man used to hold up during his frequent sermons condemning all other religions? Maybe.

He was always holding up cards with everything from the "peace symbol" to the "gay pride flag," saying they were all REALLY marks of the devil. I think he may have once even said the old Texaco logo was an old witchcraft symbol combined with a kind of cross. My memory is fuzzy about some of these things.

As the sky gets darker, the torches become the main illumination here. The chanting and the drumming get steadily faster.

In four spots around the circle, two men and two women turn their chanting from simple "Ah ah ah"s to specific words, in unison, in a language I don't know.

It's getting even darker. And creepier. And louder.

We should have tried to run from here before this. Even though the hunky bodyguards would have caught us.

What the Girl's role will be in this ceremony is as unknown to me as my own role. She's standing up straight, defiantly, with a steely gaze toward the old man. I try to do the same.

As the chanting and the drumming reach a more furious pace, I realize I can hear nothing from outside the circle. No planes flying above us. No cars on any surrounding roads. Not even any barking dogs.

I can't see outside the circle either, except up to the starry night sky. And yes, there's a full moon up there.

I close my eyes as the din increases. I silently pray to the Lord. I tell Him I can't really be meant to be the Antichrist's receptacle, just as I wasn't meant to be the "catalyst" for that alternative Rapture. I ask the Lord to show me what to do to prevent the regular old Rapture. Or at least to protect me. Or at least to keep me (relatively) calm and sane.

I open my eyes, startled, when the chanting and the drumming instantly stop, by the vocal command of the beefy bodyguards.

The old man, who had been stooped over when I first re-met him, is now standing up straight. His voice has the old fiery countenance as he shouts into his microphone.

"We are here on this night to hasten the arrival of God's glorious kingdom, by unleashing the Great Storm upon the world, in the form of Satan incarnate.

"This man you see before you will be the great demon's host body in this world. He will have fame and renown. He will have a successful career in religion and politics. Millions will love, respect, and, most of all, obey him. He will lead unknowing followers of Christ down the path of temptation, into the lust for wealth and for power. He will encourage the sins of war, of destruction, of hatred, of crime. And he will claim to be doing all of this in the name of our Lord and savior.

"Then when, with his help, the world and the human race can no longer survive on their own, Gideon's mighty trumpet will sound. The Lord God will descend to earth, with the angels, on a fleet of golden chariots. Those of us who have remained faithful to the true Christianity will rule with God in this new world.

"Yes, the great build-up to that glorious day begins at this moment, at this place.

Come now. All of you. I beseech you. Bring this to pass! Summon the Dark Angel into this space, into this host! Let the Time of Tribulation begin!"

Each of the special chanters on opposite points of this circle (roughly north-south and east-west) shouts, one after another, a high-pitched shriek that may or may not contain words spoken in a strange language. Each shriek is punctuated by a BOOM-BOOM from the drummers.

Each of the two beefy bodyguards then adds to the shrieks.

Then the old man himself shouts (as strongly as he can in his condition) into his microphone.

"Prepare the transference!"

The male "special" chanters at the "north and south" points of the circle slowly walk toward the Girl. With one of them on each side of her, they prompt her to turn her around to face me.

The old man speaks again.

"This lass, this brazen hussy, has previously hosted the spirit of the Evil One, in a less concentrated form. She is the perfect one to receive Satan's essence and transfer it to the Chosen Vessel. Begin the summoning!"

The two men perform some sort of creepy dance around the girl, waving their arms up and down. The drummers resume pounding at their top speed. Individuals around the circle make high and low shrieks.

After about a minute, maybe two, the drummers suddenly stop

again. The chanters stop. The men dancing around the girl stop.

The Girl stares into my eyes with a deadly serious glare. She, or whoever she's become, Means Business.

The two female "special" chanters at the "east" and "west" points of the circle now walk toward me.

The old man now proclaims, "Now we bring forth the Master of Darkness from this intermediary vessel into his new, permanent, corporeal host. Begin the transference!"

I feel unable to move from my spot. I seem to have been placed into a trance without my even knowing it. Am I really this easily used? I make a silent prayer to the Lord to protect me from whatever will happen, whether this rite really could bring Hell on Earth or not.

The two women lead me by the hand. I feel myself walking toward the center of the circle. I can't turn my head, but I can hear the two men leading the girl here before I can see her.

The two women and two men now bring the girl and I face to face. It takes just a simultaneous nudge on their part to bring the girl and I forward to where we're touching. The two women hold and guide my head. The two men hold and guide the girl's head. They lead us into a kissing position. We both feel compelled to enact what could be called the ultimate "kiss of death."

She reaches toward me with her lips. Mine reach out to meet hers.

There's a noise, a commotion from outside the circle.

Someone runs into the circle, screaming like a proverbial Banshee.

The torches held by the people in the circle don't spread much light out here to the center. So I don't immediately see who this person is.

It seems to be a woman. A low-voiced, rather muscular woman.

Fully nude. (Though in the limited light, with her frenetic dance moves, it's hard to see her body in much detail.)

Where have I seen her short, curly, blonde hair before?

Without a microphone, she shouts so all can hear.

"YOU FOOLS!

"You believe you can summon Satan to submit to your bidding, with this rickety sham of an invocation?

"I say you cannot! FOR I AM SATAN. The true Satan. The angel who aspires to become a god. NOT the Satan of your confused religious doctrine. Not the lord of evil, but the lord of transformation! Not the prince of darkness, but the prince of light! Lord and servant, woman and man, spiritual and carnal, all at once!

"You say you seek to bring the spirit of your 'Antichrist' into this world?

"I say you CANNOT!

"Because that spirit is already here!

"It is within you, all of you! It is within men and women through-out Christendom, throughout the world. Waging war in the name of the Prince of Peace. Loving thy neighbor, except when that neighbor's skin is a different shade than yours, or when that neighbor loves different things, or gods, or people, than you do.

"End this foolishness NOW! BE GONE!"

She takes the Girl and I in each of her hands as she runs out of the circle.

I only briefly glimpse the old man and his followers, standing around out of their previous formation, looking around, confused.

Seconds later, by the red convertible out at the front of this lot, the woman who'd driven up here with the skinny-fingered man puts her wig back on. I help the skinny-fingered man re-strap his chest with Ace bandages.

The Girl's trying to hot-wire another car parked out here. She's not making much progress here in the dark.

I can't see them, but I can hear some of the Old Man's followers scrambling toward us.

The skinny-fingered man also hears them, and climbs into the convertible, still only half dressed. The woman whistles for the girl to forget about that car and to get into this one.

With the man driving, we speed away at full blast.

After he's been driving us a while, the skinny-fingered man finally speaks directly to me.

"I couldn't have done this if I weren't still pre-op."

I tell him he no longer has to try to be an alpha male. He's proven he is one. "Active, for good," as my female co-pastor would say.

It's well after dark Tuesday. We're back on the road, for what I hope is the last time.

We had one minor scare just after we'd started. We saw a county sheriff's car with its siren and lights blazing. The driver HAD been speeding earlier; and, due to the hurry we were in when we took off, he wasn't fully dressed.

Our driver pulled over; but the cop car passed us. The skinny fingered man then said he'd better pull over for a moment. While he got his pants, shoes, and suit jacket back on, I looked out the rear view window to see if anyone from the old man's rapture cult were after us. I saw no one.

Once again in his full male garb, the man driving this convertible got back in and started back out.

The man and the woman who loves him are now singing a song together, a cappella. It's a song about loving someone, forever, no matter what happens in one's life.

After the song is done, the woman tells me and the girl I'm with that she can't wait for him to fully be a man. She says she still loves him as he is, with the help of a handy strap-on, but will love him more when he finally and fully becomes his true self.

Then the woman tells us why she wears a wig. She'd met him at a hospital support group. She's been through chemo. She's had removed, involuntarily, what he will soon have removed, voluntarily. Unfortunately, he can't give his to her. It doesn't work that way, she says; "it's not like organ donation. Even though, technically, they ARE organs."

Have I ever met a more devoted-to-each-other couple? My parents sure didn't end up that way.

We're now finally back on the freeway. That everywhere/nowhere, which comforts me but terrifies the girl beside me. Or at least it used to. I look at her now. She doesn't seem TOO scared now.

Instead, she looks relaxed, relieved. She's leaning back here in the back seat. She's silently mouthing out some alt-rock song. She seems half asleep, even though her eyes are open. I hope to spend many more nights beside her as she sleeps.

Her cell phone is currently on top of the dashboard, powering up thanks to an in-car charger. The woman and man here don't seem to have a connector for that gadget that fits my phone, however.

Now, we pass the city (and the abandoned beer factory) named for the city of the ancient gods.

I take as a cue to ask the skinny-fingered man if it's true what he'd said about Satan really being an angel of transformation, of becoming like gods. He said yeah, it was some bit of standard Wicca teaching he'd picked up at a "trans support" group once.

Another set of mysteries I don't want to get into right now.

The Girl hears me talking with the man, sits up straight, and starts talking about trying to sort out what she and I have been through these past four days. Like how everything we did to escape just brought us back in to the mess. She says it's sort of like the old "Pac-Man" maze, where you exit out the right side and just re-enter on the left side.

Now that's a set of mysteries I will need to get into, though not necessarily tonight.

But it gets me thinking:

Is this interlocking web of conspiracies and cults we've been through even bigger and more complex than we've seen?

And doesn't ANYBODY want to stay on this planet and work to try and make it better?

And what the (F-word) do my co-pastors have to do with this, beyond supplying hormone meds to the skinny-fingered man?

We've now driven past a big, protected "wetlands." We're passing the main exit for a big military base, at the south edge of a place that used to call itself the "City of Destiny."

I've heard enough conflicting claims about my supposed destiny to last at least a few lifetimes. I don't want to hear any more any time soon.

The woman asks the Girl what she'll do now.

The girl says she wants to start her life over again, in her old hometown, with or without the help of her "quote-unquote real family." She wants to be at least one state line away from her past life, with the booze and the weed and the meth and the other things.

The woman reminds her that all those things are just about

everywhere in America these days. The Girl says if she's away from the places and people she connects with her old habits, it'll be easier for her to stay away from those habits. At least she hopes so.

I know what I want her to do. I want her to be with me. Despite our age difference, across the old adulthood threshold.

She's 21, at least, I think. I'd first thought she was younger than my older sister. Then I'd thought she was older. I don't know for sure. I still don't believe I've asked her yet.

But I'm over the age of consent in this state (obviously, since I'm a licensed driver). Our relationship is legal.

But my mother and sister might still disapprove.

Well, tough.

There's a time when everybody has to take control of his or her own life, and not just ride along with someone else driving, as it were. The girl and I are together, and that's that.

Then the woman in the front seat asks me what I'm going to do.

I realize I haven't thought that through, beyond getting through high school and being there for the girl I'm with.

Most immediately, what will I tell my mother about where I've been and what I've done?

We've now passed the big mall south of the biggest city on this route. Through the city itself, with its factories and its stadiums and its skyscrapers and its official symbol tower that represents both feminine curve and masculine thrust at once. Past the big lake in the middle of the city, the university campus, another mall, yet another mall.

Past the roof lights of the jet plane factory, the largest building by volume in the world. Past the old "mill town."

Past another wetlands, and a couple of very small marinas.

Off of the freeway at the row of gas stations and the casino where a drive-in theater had apparently been decades ago.

Through the vestigial little run-down town that's now mostly the administrative center for the surrounding sprawl.

Out the other side of the old town, down a gently curving country road, with its own periodic memorial signs to people killed by drunk drivers.

Up to the subdivision entrance that used to have a big wooden sign that announced SUNNYSIDE HILLS.

I tell the skinny-fingered man and the woman at his side that the Girl and I can get out right here. I thank them again for everything; the Girl does likewise.

The red convertible makes a U-turn and then drives back off, back toward the freeway.

The convertible's fading engine noise is the only sound I hear, aside from my and the Girl's breathing.

This place is normally quiet at night, but it's not THIS quiet.

30.
WHERE IS EVERYBODY?
WHY IS EVERYBODY HERE?

The Girl and I set off on foot through Sunnyside Hills, on the subdivision's familiar sidewalk-less roads, past the driveways with kids' bikes and toys strewn about, past the cars parked in driveways (one on blocks), past the yard signs for two-month-old political campaigns.

I warn her it's an old rambler-house subdivision, not a modern luxury McMansion tract; though she can see that now. I also tell her it looks better at night, when it looks a little more mysterious, a little less just plain ugly.

She says it looks like a great place to rebel against. She says she could just imagine herself as a kid here, hating the stifling all-American blandness of it all. She says they're probably all TV-addled hicks who've never knowingly read a book or eaten a vegetable.

While I'm glad to see her getting more of her sardonic verve back, I try to tell her it's not really that bad, not really. I tell her the people here are mostly nice people, except for the mean ones. We've got immigrant families from Morocco and Ghana, and retired sawmill workers with only three fingers on each hand, and a lesbian couple with four dogs, and a black athletic coach married to a white legal assistant, and really just about every kind of person—except people who can afford to live someplace nicer.

Our footsteps, breaths, and voices are literally the only sound out here.

There are usually dogs barking outside these houses, day and night. I wonder why I don't hear any.

I also don't hear any TV shows, or streaming music, or video game sounds from inside the thin-walled, under-insulated, cheaply built houses.

It's not THAT late; the clock on the Girl's recharged phone proves it. Not even eleven.

Everything is dark and still here in the subdivision, except for the streetlights and the lights in the houses.

The stars are brighter than normal. Is the "super moon" related to this? I just don't know.

After a left and two rights, we reach the cul-de-sac my house is on. The house to the left of ours, from outside of which normally you can hear anything from loud laughing to loud arguing to loud sex, is as quiet as the other houses.

I show the Girl the front of my house. It's no bigger or smaller than any of them here, with a two-car garage that makes it seem a little bigger than it is. The outside was painted a weird institutional beige just last year. I remember the name on the paint cans as something weird like "Verbena Herbal Tea." The paint hides a couple of worn out spots in the siding; my mother always says she'll spring for new wall coverings "next year."

No vehicles are parked in the driveway. But that's not so strange. My mother's old Sentra, and my sister's even older hand-me-down Camry (almost as old as she is) are sometimes parked in the driveway and sometimes in the garage.

The small front lawn I've mowed too many times to think about.

The Girl sees a small yard sign stuck into the lawn, warning that the property's protected by some name-brand security alarm system. I tell her it isn't really; we just bought the sign at a drugstore.

While most of the other houses here have lights on tonight, no lights are on at my family's house. Not even the front porch light. Odd. Are my mother and sister out somewhere looking for me?

I knock on the door. No answer. Not unexpected, with the lights off.

I reach into my pants pocket and take out the key chain that I got back when I got back my original clothes.

The front door key doesn't work.

I lead the girl around the side yard (I think they call it a "setback") to the back door. The key for that one also doesn't work.

Have the locks been changed? Would my mother have done that without telling me? (Not that she's had the chance to tell me these past few days.)

We go to the front of the house again. The garage door key also doesn't work.

Now THIS is getting weird, I tell the Girl. She just shrugs it off; we've both been through even weirder things lately.

I tell her there's one last way in. It's through a bedroom window. My sister always keeps hers open—probably to keep the weed smell from going into the rest of the house. I assure the Girl with me that I've never barged in on my sister in her room. Not before now, anyway. But since it's the only thing I can think of doing....

The window's higher than either of us can reach. I try to lift the girl up. I can't do it. She tries to lift me up. That works.

The door's open just a bit. I slide it open further.

Struggling, I lift myself up and pull myself through. I tell the girl to meet me at the back door.

It's all dark in here. And, yes, it's silent.

I jump down from the windowsill to the floor, as silently as I can (not very).

There's nobody in my sister's room. Her bed is made. Her usual bedroom stuff is, from a quick glance in the darkness, all here.

I walk slowly through the dark, short hallway, to the dark, small kitchen.

It's odd to find it this dark, this quiet, this empty, this devoid of life.

But it's still my home. The home I've tried for days to get back to. With the Girl's help. Against all sorts of obstacles. Despite at least two more-or-less attempts on my life, and some other moments of peril, and a lot of just plain not knowing what the fuck was going on.

Hmm: I'm not censoring my own thoughts right now. Does that mean something? Probably not.

But I'm home. The journey's end. Waves of tension drop from my shoulders. I let my tiredness, my hunger, and my sore muscles reveal themselves to me.

Before I turn on any lights, I get to the kitchen door and let the Girl in.

She comes in. She doesn't move to turn any lights on either.

I sense a presence in here. I mean, besides the Girl and myself. But I ignore it for now.

Before I do anything else, I kiss her, in my own kitchen, in the dark.

I've made it.

No, WE'VE made it.

I whisper in her ear that I couldn't have done it without her. She was right all along: I needed her. And I still do.

Just then, a single light comes on from the adjacent living room.

I turn around and see the infinitely welcome face of my mother.

She's not dressed in her usual late-night attire (bathrobe, fake silk PJs, tan bedroom slippers). Instead, she's got her best work clothes on.

I expect her to jump up and hug me, and tell me she'd been so worried about me, and tell me not to talk just yet because there will be time for that later, but who's this young woman with me and did she drive me home and does either her or me need a bite to eat.

She doesn't do any of that.

She remains seated.

Her expression is a simple, businesslike smile. Just like the ones she uses in her bank-teller job.

My sister sits next to her on the couch. She's dressed in one of her own best outfits, one she's worn to job interviews. She gives a polite smile to the Girl and then to me.

My mother speaks, in an unusually formal, "sing-song-y" tone of voice.

"We were expecting you HOURS ago, my dear. What in the WORLD has kept you? You really should have let us know. Was it the traffic? I know it can get bad at this time of year, what with the slick roads and the visibility in the rain."

Now she looks at the girl.

"Oh, so YOU'RE the one they've been telling me about. The wild card, the one who's put all our careful plans into chaos over and over. You seem to be just as spunky and industrious as they say you are. How HAS my dear boy been treating you? I just KNOW you two MUST have had a pleasant few days together. My dear boy is SUCH the perfect gentleman, don't you agree? Honestly, can there be a sweeter, more polite young man anywhere?"

The Girl looks at me. She takes off one of her pure-black earrings and hands it to me. She says it contains a little transmitter, that had helped "these people" to find us wherever we went.

Breaking her "tough girl" image completely, she begins to weep, then sob. What she says isn't completely clear, but it seems to include, "Believe me. PLEASE. I tried to stop them. I tried to protect you. I tried to save you. Please believe me! Please!"

Then, as my eyes adjust to the light, I see more people in the room.

A lot more.

How could they ALL be here?

They don't even all know each other.

Or do they?

31.
WHO AM I?
WHAT AM I?
AM I?

It's less than an hour later. My body systems, which had almost OD'd several times in recent days on the high from "fight or flight" hormones, seem to be approaching full rest as a withdrawal symptom. I seem unable to bring them back up, now that I need them the most.

I've been taken, restrained, placed face-up on a table.

The girl's restrained next to me. From here, I can't tell if she's on this same table or an adjacent one. Not that it matters.

She's feistier than I am right now. She's squirming, stretching her restraints, and trying to break free. I should follow her lead. But I can't, somehow. Am I really this susceptible to induced trances, to other people's desires for me?

We're both in the clothes we wore when we came in here. Only our jackets were removed.

She's said several times during this ordeal that she was on "my side." But how's she really connected to this whole scheme? What did she know, and when did she know it?

And does that matter now?

Yes. It does.

Truth matters.

Not what I or anyone else believes to be true, but what really IS true.

There IS such a thing as Reality. The Reality that exists whether you believe in it or not.

That's not what the people surrounding us are saying. They're talking, orating, and chanting, about creating a "new truth," a "new world".

They're talking about reshaping the present, the future, even the past, by their connections to higher entities.

They're dressed in their own notions of what in church we used to call their "Sunday best." It's clearly a major occasion for them all.

We're in the garage of my family's house. Where the family's two cars are, I don't know, and it doesn't matter.

(Am I finally learning to only think about what matters, without all these side tangents I usually get?)

Black curtains have been put up on the walls in here.

The only light here comes from a lot of candles (at least a hundred by my guess), placed all around the room, on iron candle holders of various heights.

From where I am I can't see everyone in this space. But I can hear them.

The woman the Girl calls "Pseudo-Mom" is chanting something smooth and steady, if unemotionally.

Pseudo-Mom's partner, the Angry Man, is vocalizing far more aggressively.

The Energy Healer Dude is mumbling his vocal part.

The ménage-a-trois farmers are vocalizing in sync with each other, but out of sync with the rest of the people here.

The female militia pimp sounds like she's got a much more trained voice than most of the others. She's performing her vocal part in a true, steady, impassioned monotone, like a tribal rite.

Her husband, the muscular male militia pimp, is so silent, he's almost mouthing his notes.

I can't see whether the old Naked Guy from the "intentional community" camp is naked now. He's shrieking at appropriate and inappropriate points in the overall chant.

The Town Mistress from the same camp is moaning, in a low, gravelly tone of voice.

I don't hear or see the Old Man from the Rapture cult, but I hear his burly bodyguards with their booming voices.

The chemo-patient woman with a wig is barely in sight of me. She's singing like a choir soprano.

The skinny-fingered man, in the same suit I'd last seen him in, is alternating low- and high-tenor choruses.

Just what they're all performing is unknown to me. It's not like the total cacophony of the ascension orgy cult; and it's not like the loud but solemn incantation of the Rapture cult. It's more of a harmonious, somehow coordinated noise, a patiently slow noise. Some of it sounds low, like a throbbing synth sample or really low microphone feedback. Some of it sounds high, almost to dog-whistle territory (can human voices even do that?). The middle tones just massage my head and body with their constant ebb and flow. It begins in time to sound both very familiar and very strange.

I see the old woman from the ascension cult, still in her flowing rainbow robe, still with her thick-bottomed walking stick. She pounds it on the floor, in rhythm with the blended vocals, as she contributes her own operatic sounding trills to the mix.

My older sister, whom I'd really thought better of, stands near my left shoulder. She's silent, but she's making various interpretive dance moves from the waist up. What part did SHE have in all this? I might never know.

My mother stands near my right shoulder. She makes no sounds or movements. She just beams at me with some weird sense of matronly pride. I don't have to look at her for long before the sight disgusts me.

I hear the door from the garage to the rest of the house open and close. I hear two sets of footsteps approach me. I hear the various vocalizers soften their output, then pause it.

I hear two familiar, but now frightening, voices.

Both my co-pastors stand near my head. They lean over so I can see their faces. They grin even more sickeningly than my mother.

My attention's really is starting to fade now. I don't quite make out what my co-pastors are saying; taking turns speaking one sentence at a time. But I think it goes something like:

"Behold, the new Ascended One."

"The new lodestar to guide humanity through its forthcoming era of great tribulation."

"Bred and reared to be pure of mind and heart."

I glance at my mother, who grins even more maniacally.

The co-pastors continue.

"Raised to have a moral compass, to wish for a world that was better than this one."

"Intelligent, well-spoken, courteous."

"Wise beyond his years."

Now even my sister's grinning disgustingly.

The co-pastors go on.

"Then, to ensure he was prepared, he was sent through a rapid succession of tests."

"Each test was devised to test him in a different way, to test a different aspect of his soul."

"And though every aspect of these tests did not transpire as planned..." They look disapprovingly at the girl, restrained beside me. She gives them a silent raspberry and mouths a silent "fuck this."

"...Still, our subject proved himself, time and again, to be more than capable."

"He endangered his own freedom to help someone in need."

"He refused a life of safety and seclusion, instead choosing to be out in the world, to be an active worker for good."

"He helped people he'd known, and also people he hadn't known."

"Rising above the narrow doctrinal teachings of his childhood, he came to the aid of some of society's castoffs."

"Setting his male ego aside, he repeatedly listened to, and heeded, a woman's instructions."

"Recruiting others to assist him, when he knew he could not perform the deed alone, he disrupted an exercise intended to bring deliberate evil into further dominance in our world."

"And, rejecting the fleeting pleasures of the flesh, he opted to assist, protect, and prove his devotion to a fellow human soul."

"He has proven himself ready."

"And now we are also ready."

"He will become the newest of the ascended masters, the living spirits of the great I AM."

"The spirits who guide the grand overall direction of the universe."

"And the spirits who also aid lost individuals, people on this dimension who need guidance toward happiness and prosperity in harmony with the grand designs."

"These spirits often appear in visions to the living in the form of adolescent boys, wise and innocent at once."

Did she say "to the living," as if I would no longer be "living" myself?

"The lore has shown us the path to becoming an Ascended One."

"To pass into the next dimension, without the soul-damaging violence that comes with physical death."

Oh no. Not THAT again.

What's with this obsession among these people, anyway?

"And now, we also present a second soul to join him."

"Someone who has proven herself a worthy soul mate."

"Courageous, defiant, never defeated; her instinctual sense complements his deliberate training."

Oh NO. They're sacrificing HER TOO?

For what? To be the Adam and Eve of the spirit world, populating some new plane of existence or whatever?

Fuck this. FUCK THIS!

If I could say it aloud, I would.

Why can't I?

The co-pastors look, and stretch their arms, upward.

"Beings of the next dimension: receive these offerings to your world with grace and dignity."

"Teach and nurture them as well as we have attempted to."

Now the co-pastors spread their arms out above me, toward the others in this garage.

"Let it be made so!"

Instead of a chaotic array of voices, the people around the garage unite to create one unified set of tones, with harmonious overtones and undertones. Every person, every voice, every vocal range, somehow meshes together. I can't tell if they're singing anything with, you know, words.

As the ritual continues, I feel myself less able to fully hear it. The sound becomes one combined chord, then one note, then a blur.

I don't close my eyes, but my sight goes away anyway. Instead of specific people in a specific room, I see patterns of light. Circles inside of other circles. Waves. Splotches of color.

My clothes seem to drop off from my body.

My body dissolves into pure Spirit.

The patterns and sounds leave me.

Everything leaves me.

I am truly alone.

Everything is completely dark.

Then everything becomes lighter.

A hazy, diffuse light, but a light still.

The whole realm of human existence, the trivialities and the meaningless ambitions and even individual identities, begins to seem both foolish and distant, like observing the mating habits of houseflies.

I feel my mind getting hazier, less able to remember, less able to form thoughts.

I seem to be becoming a being of pure consciousness. No here/there, no past/present/future. Even language is leaving me.

I realize that my next thought, my next vision, may be my last, at least in this earthly identity.

That thought won't be about my mother. Not after she turned out to have betrayed me, my whole life.

No, it will be about the one who stayed with me through all of this. Who may have also had a role in the staging of my ordeal, but who said she'd tried to save me. And I believe her.

I have enough mental strength to focus on my memory of her

voice. Her face. Her fighting spirit. Her refusal to let things "just happen."

Her way of telling the world off with one huge "FUCK THIS!"

Even without an aural voice, I shout it to the heavens: FUCK THIS! FUCK THIS! FUCK THIS!

FUCK!

THIS!

As I keep mentally screaming it out, everything changes.

32.
I KNOW THE ANSWERS.
OR SOME OF THEM ANYWAY.
I KNOW MORE THAN THEY THINK I KNOW.

Thoughts are forming more easily in my mind now.

The blurry white light is now a little more formed, in circles and ovals of various colors.

The music is becoming more distinct, more differentiated. It takes on different rhythms, different keys, and different tones. I hear a couple of different "beep beep beep" rhythms, and a whooshing of air that sounds a little like Darth Vader's breathing. "Industrial," I think they call this genre.

There are also vocalizations, several different ones. If they're singing or chanting anything specific, I can't tell what it is.

I'm definitely "in my body" again. At least partly. I can feel the sore points in my body from my ordeals. In some moments some of these sore points flare into dull pains, then fade back.

I feel an urge to Do Something. What, I don't know.

Then I feel a counter-urge to be patient, to let whatever happens, happen.

But I remember that "letting what happens, happen" is how I got into this state, this condition, this whatever-it-is.

I try, again, to concentrate on one thing.

That one thing, again, is the "girl" (really a young woman) who'd been at my side.

Her attitude. Her fight. Her refusal to just "let what happens, happen."

I can, should, must be more like that. More like her.

If I were more like her, what would I do now?

I'd fight, that's what.

But what does "fighting" mean, in my current whatever-it-is?

I decide it means fighting for reality. The real reality, not the "make your own reality" reality.

The reality that sometimes hurts. A lot.

The reality that's full of confusion, misunderstanding, ignorance.

The reality that contains cruelty, mistakes, imperfections.

The reality that's neither Heaven nor Hell, but the just plain Here and Now.

The light and color patterns in my vision become yet more distinct. Some of them shrink in size, from big and blurry to small and specific.

The "music" I hear becomes less like "music" and more like just plain "sounds." I can tell they're coming from several different sources.

The "vocalizations" I hear become less like "singing" and more like "talking." I still can't grasp what they're saying. There are too many voices at once. It's hard to tell them apart.

I can sense the different parts of my body. My left arm feels punctured, with a foreign object penetrating it. My mouth and nose seem to have things of some sort on them. My torso has something clinging to it. I still don't feel my legs.

Individual voices are becoming clearer to me. I begin to hear what they're saying. I don't understand it, but I hear it. At least some of it. Sounds become syllables, which become words, which become sentences, which I can at least partly "get":

"...whether to live or..."

"...processing his life so far, and what his life will be if he..."

"...they do have them, sometimes. Vivid ones. We didn't used to think so, but new research shows that...."

"...adolescent-boy obsessions. Breaking out from his parents. Finding his way in the world. Finding his life's purpose. What it means to 'become a man.'" Dealing with females. Probably a lot about dealing..."

"...improved vitals. Holding steady for the past..."

"...ideal mate. Not just a sex partner, but someone with qualities he feels he needs but doesn't..."

"...probably because the church felt like another family to..."

"...almost died. Three, maybe four, times. But now the worst might be..."

"...horrible, terrible minister they used to have. Harmed so many..."

"...-ing of life, at least so far as an 11th grader can under-..."

"...his age, just about any female's essentially an authority fig..."

"...good driver, just inexperienced. He didn't know how to react to..."

"...like they're in this whole other dimension, existing at a lower vibration, a lower energy level, trying to get back to..."

"...had more friends. But his mannerisms, his formal, stilted speech pat-..."

"...my fault. All of it. If only I hadn't asked him to go to the camp separately, in my own..."

"...what other boys like. Not video games, not action movies, not even normal teenage swear..."

"...can hear more than we think they..."

"...seemed so distant at times. Like he was barely inside his own bo..."

"...their way back home, however they define..."

"...lost? Really? That far from where the camp..."

"...to blame ANYBODY. Except that drunken..."

"...has any sense of decency, he's probably in a world of hurt right..."

"...so obsessed with all my own drama, when I could have been a better sister to..."

"...thought it was a woman driving that..."

The words fade back into an unintelligible blah-blah-blah. Then they fade out altogether.

I feel my mind re-aligning, "rewiring," as it were.

Thoughts that were central to me, obsessive even, are not only fading, I'm forgetting what they were.

I don't want to forget.

I won't forget.

I try to think up "keywords," as they say in web-design class at school.

Words I can repeat to myself as my mind goes into its next state, or condition, or whatever-it-is.

Locked trunk. Skinny fingers. Curly Wig. Southern Comfort. "Out of Your League." Black Earrings. Breast Tattoo. Angry Man. Pseudo-Mom. Burrito. Beaver Springs. Trojan Park. Cold House. Itchy Blanket. Special Sugar. Huge Tent. Rainbow Robe. Walking Stick. Ascension Orgy. Running Naked. Camp Philomath. Black Dress. Kalama. Six Drinks. Weird Therapy. Healer Dude. Broken Cars. Grand Mound. Red Pickup. Mr. and Mrs. Goon Squad. McMansion. Target Range. Mima Mounds. Off the Grid. Tiny House. Mushroom Man. Naked Santa Guy. Town Mistress. Wooden Shed. Red Convertible. Highest Bidder. Rapture Cult. Old Man. Summoning the Antichrist. Satan Woman. Pre-Op. The Girl. The Girl. The Girl.

Words to help me remember everything I've been through.

Everything I KNOW I've been through.

I suspect people will tell me it didn't really happen.

They'll tell me my recent "reality" wasn't the "real" reality.

But I know better.

I still know better.

I still repeat the "keywords" in my mind, as well as I can continue to remember them all, as my hearing comes back into focus. As my eyes flutter open. As I see, and feel, the oxygen hose on my nostrils, the IV in my arm, the Ace bandages around my upper torso.

A woman dressed in "scrubs" and a surgical mask asks if I can feel or move my legs or feet.

It takes a second to understand what she's saying, what she's asking for.

When I do understand it, I try to move the toes on my left foot, then on my right foot.

I can't feel them, but the doctor (I presume that's who she is) says I succeeded.

I recognize the beep-beep-beep of different machines in this room, at different pitches and rhythms.

The doctor decides I can only handle one visitor at a time.

My mother, of course, is first.

She's all weepy and smiley and all. She tells me to take my sweet time getting better, and when I come home I can eat "regular teenager food" if I want to, and I can wait to go back to school until I really feel like it, and they'll put all the rehab stuff I might need into my room, and that I should just become my own sweet self and I'll be all better in no time flat.

The sister's next. I see her talking to what must be her "boyfriend du jour" in the hallway before she enters my room. He looks way too old for her. (Wait: What am I saying?)

Anyway, she says she's been praying for me even though she doesn't go to church anymore, and promises to be a better friend to me from now on. She gushes over me and tries to hug me; but my arms are still strapped into this bed.

Next to enter are the co-pastors.

The male co-pastor says the youth group camp weekend just wasn't the same without me, that all the kids in the group sent their well wishes and prayers, that he hadn't told the other kids right away that I'd gone missing before they found the wrecked car (with me in it) in a ditch out in the countryside.

This is the first I've heard of what happened to me. No: what these people want me to believe happened to me.

He also says if I can find it in my heart to ever forgive the drunk man or woman who'd run into me (he says they're still not sure who was driving that car at the time), it would be a great step toward my spiritual growth. But then he says I don't have to think about that right now. (Then why did he mention it?)

The female co-pastor enters next. She gushes over me even more than my family did. She says I really, REALLY shouldn't worry about the car. The insurance will handle it. (Was I even worrying about the car?)

She then says she was SO frightened when she first heard I hadn't made it to the camp. She pleads with me to forgive her for having sent me out separately to the camp in her car. She says she should have been more protective than she'd been, but I just had seemed so mature for my age.

She doesn't mention anything about our Friday-night affair. Well, she wouldn't, what with her husband right outside in the hall. Is that going to be something she, and everyone else, will try to tell me never happened?

By running my own set of "keywords" in my head over and over, I'm determined to remember that, and everything else. As I concentrate on remembering them, the female co-pastor remarks that I'm being distant and inattentive. But she adds that that's probably to be expected. She tells me to keep the faith and keep getting better. She leaves the room without even a romantic wink.

A wall-mounted, flat-screen TV in the room shows a series of text screens, displaying announcements of this day's hospital activities. There's a listing for a support group for breast cancer survivors, and another group for gender-reassignment patients and their loved ones. There's a seminar on frontiers in energy healing techniques. There are AA and NA meetings, for adults and teens. There's a woman from the southwest corner of the state coming up here to introduce a new technique in physical therapy.

Another TV here is showing a local newscast, with the sound muted but with the closed captioning turned on. There are stories about the criminal link between a survivalist camp and a sex-trafficking ring; about the fad for "tiny houses;" about a local Native tribe fighting for federal recognition; and about how climate change might affect lowlands and shorelines around the region.

Is this some big campaign to "gaslight" me into disbelieving what happened to me?

Could it be that I wasn't dreaming then but I am now?

Could I have been really, involuntarily, "ascended" into another dimension, where this is all being staged, performed to mold and shape me somehow?

Or, could they have succeeded in altering "reality" itself using my spirit, then changed history to put me into this condition?

Maybe I was wrong about competing "realities."

Maybe there really are people who can shape and mold "realities" for themselves and others, for good or ill.

It's so confusing.

And I'm tired, and (it turns out) foggy on pain meds.

Or so says the nursing assistant who's in the room now. She wears pitch-black earrings. She wears a T-shirt that looks vaguely like a baseball jersey under her uniform. From some angles, she looks to be in her late 20s or early 30s. From other angles, she looks to be my age, or even a little younger.

She leans over toward my face. She tells me, simply, quietly, "I know. And I'll help you. You don't know it but you need me."

I interrupt silently reciting my "keywords" just long enough to tell her, simply, quietly, "I know."

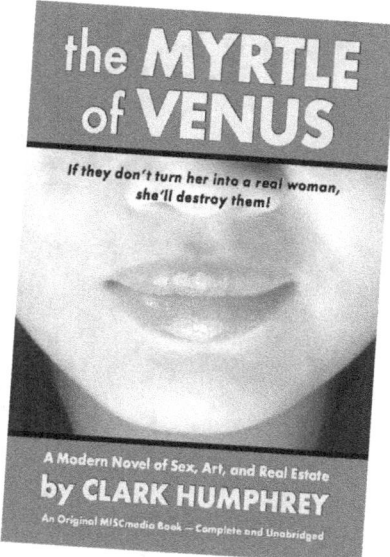